## "I want to celebrate…"

"What are we celebrating?" [...] asked.

"My birthday," Pippa said. "I'm twenty-five today."

"Happy birthday, Pippa."

The band was playing and he noticed that Pippa swayed to the music. "So, Pippa, what are we going to do?"

She arched one eyebrow at him. "I'm not sure what you mean. What are we going to do about what?"

"This night," he said. He put his hand on her waist and drew her closer to him.

"I'm not sure," she said softly.

Her breath smelled sweet, like the prosecco they'd drunk, and her face was so close that his lips tingled, remembering how soft and succulent they had been beneath his.

"Well, I'm yours…for tonight," he said out loud to remind himself that it was only for this night. "Tell me what it is you want me to do."

She tipped her head back and their eyes met. Her lips parted and he felt her hand come to rest on his shoulder. "Show me a good time, cowboy."

\* \* \*

*Rancher Untamed* is part of the Cole's Hill Bachelors series from *USA TODAY* bestselling author Katherine Garbera!

Dear Reader,

I'm really excited to be telling Pippa's story at last! From the moment she showed up on the page in *Tycoon Cowboy's Baby Surprise* I was intrigued. I knew she'd run away from her family, but I didn't know all the details at first. Her bond with Kinley and with Penny showed me how compassionate she was, and in each book since then I've been learning more about her. After I finished *Craving Her Best Friend's Ex*, it made sense to tell Pippa's story as I knew her pretty well by that point.

If you've been reading my Wild Caruthers Bachelors series, you'll also recognize Diego Velasquez. He's one of Bianca's four brothers, and as the eldest has always felt a sense of legacy and heritage. He has taken over running his family's horse ranch in Cole's Hill. He is intrigued with Pippa from running into her around town, but it's not until she bids on him in the annual Cole's Hill charity bachelor auction that he gets a chance to really know her.

Neither of them intends for their night together to be anything more than that. Both of them have complicated lives, but you know how it is with love— we have no control over who we fall for (as much as it would be nice to think that we do) or when it happens. To be honest, that is one of the reasons I love writing romance stories.

I hope you enjoy Pippa and Diego's story.

Happy reading!

*Katherine Garbera*

# KATHERINE GARBERA

---

## RANCHER UNTAMED

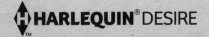

Recycling programs
for this product may
not exist in your area.

ISBN-13: 978-1-335-97181-4

Rancher Untamed

Copyright © 2018 by Katherine Garbera

**Printed in U.S.A.**

*USA TODAY* bestselling author **Katherine Garbera** writes emotional, sexy contemporary romances. An Amazon, Barnes & Noble and iBooks bestselling author, she is also a two-time Maggie Award winner and has sold more than seven million copies of her books worldwide. She loves to hear from readers via her website, www.katherinegarbera.com.

## Books by Katherine Garbera

### Harlequin Desire

#### Sons of Privilege

*The Greek Tycoon's Secret Heir*
*The Wealthy Frenchman's Proposition*
*The Spanish Aristocrat's Woman*
*His Baby Agenda*
*His Seduction Game Plan*

#### The Wild Caruthers Bachelors

*Tycoon Cowboy's Baby Surprise*
*The Tycoon's Fiancée Deal*
*Craving His Best Friend's Ex*

#### Cole's Hill Bachelors

*Rancher Untamed*

Visit her Author Profile page at Harlequin.com, or katherinegarbera.com, for more titles.

This book is dedicated to all believers in happy endings and the power of true love.

# One

Diego Velasquez felt foolish as he stood in the wings waiting to be announced in the Five Families Country Club bachelor auction. He'd give anything to be with his horses on his ranch, Arbol Verde. He had tried to get out of participating in the annual charity event by making a huge donation, but his mom, a formidable morning newscaster on a Houston station, was on the committee and wanted to see her sons—all four of them—married. So there was no getting out of it, even though every year he and his brothers tried.

"What do you think, Diego? Got it in you to

land a huge bid?" his youngest brother, Inigo, asked.

Diego was pretty sure Inigo had toyed with the idea of making one of the women who followed him on the F1 racing circuit his temporary bride to avoid the auction. But since their beloved mama was a devout Catholic, a temporary marriage was a no-no, so he'd flown in on his G6 this morning from Japan. Luckily for Inigo the F1 was racing in Austin in two weeks' time. Or maybe unluckily, because it meant there was no excuse not to be here, he thought as he watched Inigo messing with his bow tie.

Diego turned to his other two brothers, the twins. Alejandro did some sort of social media management that had made him a millionaire and he wasn't even thirty. And Mauricio had the golden eye when it came to spotting property in neighborhoods on the cusp of becoming "it" places to live and work.

Diego was proud of them. They were all the kind of bachelors that the charity auction should be promoting. Sure, it was annoying that Mama was competitive and wanted to see the Velasquez name at the top of the fund-raising leaderboard. But at the end of the day, it was a good cause, wasn't it?

"You look like you're thinking of bolting," Mo said.

"I am," Diego admitted. But before he could make good his escape, there was a commotion on stage.

"Ethan Caruthers is making a fool of himself over some woman. He just proposed to her," Inigo said, from his spot near the curtain leading to the stage.

"Crissanne Moss," Diego said, coming over to join his youngest brother. "While you were touring the world, this has been the big news in town. Ethan and Crissanne were living together and the Carutherses thought it was leading toward marriage. But then Crissanne's ex came back from the dead. Literally. People thought he'd died in a plane crash until he showed up in town, very much alive, wanting to know what was going on between his best friend and his ex-girlfriend."

"*Dios mio*, Diego, you sound like the town gossip," Alejandro said, coming up behind him and slinging his arm over Diego's shoulders.

"Don't remind me. I had dinner with Bi and Derek last night and Ma Caruthers was there spilling the dirt," Diego said.

"Ah, well, it looks like they might be getting back together," Inigo said.

"Yeah, it does," Diego said. He'd never met a woman he'd make a fool of himself over. Not like Ethan was doing right now. But as he watched Ethan go to Crissanne and embrace her...well, it made him wonder what it would be like to find one special person to settle down with.

"You're next, Diego," the stage manager said.

"Damn," he said. His chance to run was gone.

He heard Mo chuckling evilly behind him and turned to punch him in the shoulder, only softening it at the last moment because if he started a brawl with his brothers his mom would never forgive them.

"What are you afraid of?" Mo asked. "It's just harmless fun."

Yeah, it was. But as he got older, it felt like he should be retiring from this auction, not settling in as a permanent fixture. "Nothing. You're right. It's fun."

All four brothers watched the crowd as Diego's name was announced. Alejandro elbowed him, pointing to Kinley Caruthers's nanny, Pippa. She was close to the front of the crowd, a look of anticipation lighting up her heart-shaped face.

She'd caught his eye before. The cute blonde had come to Cole's Hill two years ago when Kinley moved here. Her hair was a honey blond and she usually wore it in a ponytail, but tonight it fell to her shoulders in soft waves. Her eyes were gray, but not icy at all. It was sort of a soft gray color that made him want to tell her things that he didn't even want to admit he thought about. Which made her dangerous. Her lips were full, and normally she wore only lip gloss—yeah, he'd spent a lot of time thinking about that mouth of hers. Tonight she'd used a red lipstick that made it impossible for him to look at anything but her mouth. Which was the last thing he needed because he already thought too much about what it would be like to kiss her.

She wore a figure-hugging dress in a deep blue jewel tone that made her creamy skin look even smoother than normal. He'd known her legs were long and slim because she tended to wear leggings around town, but tonight with a pair of fancy heels on they seemed longer, endless.

He groaned.

"Stop being a baby. I swear, Diego, you are the worst at this. I know they are women and not your beloved horses, but it's not that bad," Mo said.

He glanced at his brother. "I know that. I'm not exactly afraid of women."

"Your reputation proves that," Mo said. "So what's the deal?"

Mo leaned toward the curtain with him and followed Diego's gaze.

"Oh, it's like that."

"Yeah. But she's not interested and I'm—"

"Out of time," Mo said.

"Mr. Diego Velasquez," the emcee repeated.

And Diego, with a shove from Mo, walked out onto the stage.

\* \* \*

Pippa Hamilton-Hoff rarely went out and certainly didn't get dressed up all that often. But here she was, seated at the Caruthers table for the Five Families bachelor auction. Among the descendants of the original five families who'd founded Cole's Hill, there was a friendly competition to see which one could raise the most money.

Given that all of the Caruthers brothers were married except for Ethan—and he now seemed engaged—that family's chances were slim this year. But Pippa had already had other ideas. It certainly helped that she was twenty-five today and would soon have access to her fortune. She knew exactly who she wanted to spend this birthday with.

Diego Velasquez—a long, tall Texan who looked as comfortable in his tuxedo as he did on the back of a horse. Though if she were being totally honest, she preferred to see him riding his stallion Iago. She'd been out to visit him twice with Penny, the little girl she nannied. Penny was a horse-crazy four-year-old, the daughter of Nathan Caruthers, and Diego was her de facto uncle now that his sister, Bianca, had married Dr. Derek Caruthers.

The long road that she'd been on for the last four years was almost up. She no longer had to hide who she was—an English heiress who'd run away from her controlling father and had become a nanny while on the run, trying to figure out what to do next. Now that she was twenty-five her inheritance was hers to claim and do what she wanted with. For this one night she still wanted to be young and free. To be with a man who didn't know about her fortune, who would be happy enough with Pippa the nanny.

She'd run into him enough times in town to know that it wasn't coincidence. The owner of a large ranch on the outskirts of town with an internationally acclaimed breeding program didn't have to drive into Cole's Hill at 10:00 a.m. every Monday, Wednesday and Friday to get coffee, but he did. They always chatted, and she'd been careful to not let it be more than talk, but in her heart…she wanted more. He had the kind of chocolatey-brown eyes that reminded her of drinking hot chocolate, so rich and comforting. Yet at the same time he made her feel alive…feel things that she hadn't allowed herself to even think about since she'd walked out of that party in New York City four years ago and gotten on a bus.

Since then, her life had been a lie. One big deceit where she had to keep moving, keep thinking and never let her guard down.

Until now.

Tonight.

Ethan Caruthers had done the romantic thing

and now he and Crissanne were in the corner snogging. Meanwhile, Pippa was sitting here with access to her fortune and looking up at Diego Velasquez. He wore his tuxedo with an easy grace that spoke of manners and class, but when their eyes met, she felt that zing. That sexual awareness that reminded her she was more than an heiress on the run. She was a woman with a plan tonight.

Not the one who'd hidden away for four years or the one who was afraid to claim things for herself.

No, she wanted Diego and was determined to have him.

The bidding started, and she raised her hand, increasing the bid. She just kept on until she and one of the women who worked with Diego at his ranch were the only ones left. Chantelle, Pippa thought her name was. Did Chantelle wish for a relationship that was more than boss/employee?

Pippa knew she was leaving. That as soon as the board of her family's company, House of Hamilton, read her email and accepted she was who she said she was, Cole's Hill, Texas, would be a distant memory. But she'd put aside so many things for the past four years. She'd denied herself for too long and she wasn't going to anymore. She raised her paddle and doubled the current bid, which made the emcee squeal with excitement and Diego raise his eyebrows as he looked right at her.

"I think someone definitely wants you, Diego, and unless there is another bidder who wants to top that bid…" The emcee glanced around the room, but she'd pushed the bid so high no one else raised a paddle.

For the first time since Diego walked onto the stage she was truly aware of the room and that everyone's eyes were on her. She started to sit back down, but Kinley put her hand on Pippa's butt. "Get your man, girl."

She had to smile at the way Kinley said it. Despite the fact that they had grown up in two very different worlds, Kin was a soul sister. Pippa had always believed that something stronger than co-incidence had led them to meet on that Vegas bus the day Kinley went into labor. Pippa had been riding the bus trying to figure out her next move, since she was out of cash, and Kinley had been on her way to work when her water broke.

"I guess I will," Pippa said, carefully placing her paddle on the table and going up to claim him.

It was only for tonight, but then again, she felt tonight was all she'd had. She'd had four birthdays on her own in Texas, each of them fraught with tension and confusion. Only her determination had brought her to this moment, and as she climbed up the stairs at the side of the stage and went to him, she didn't worry about any of that. As she got closer, she noticed his smile, how tonight it wasn't as bold as it usually was. But it was still sexy and charming, and she admitted to herself she was smitten.

What an old-fashioned word, but it suited her and her emotions.

She hadn't really been paying attention to the other winners, so she had no idea what to do, but Diego caught her hand and pulled her close to him. "With a bid like that, I think you deserve my everything."

Up close she realized that his brown eyes had flecks of gold in them. His lips were full, and he winked at her as he dipped her low in his arms and then brought his mouth down on hers. She stopped thinking and just let go.

Diego stood in the line at the bar watching Pippa talking to Kinley and Bianca. His sister was a former supermodel, but Pippa outshone her in his eyes. He wasn't sure what they were saying, but he noticed that Pippa smiled and laughed easily. He ordered two margaritas and then made his way back over to her.

"So I guess we shouldn't wait up for you," Kinley said as he approached.

Pippa's gaze met his and she blushed, the pink tint moving up from her décolletage to her neck.

"You'll see me when you see me," Pippa said in her very proper British accent.

She reached around Kinley and took one of the margaritas from him. He lifted his glass toward hers and took a sip before he moved to stand next to her. Kinley hugged her and went to join her husband across the room.

"Mama is very proud of the Velasquez family tonight," Bianca said.

"She should be. She did a good job raising us," Diego said. "And we are all home tonight, which you know always makes her happy."

"She's not the only one who's over the moon," Bianca said. "Benito can't wait until tomorrow morning for our family brunch. He loves his *tios*."

His nephew was four years old and had seen a lot in his short life. His father had died while racing, something that had made Diego's own mother more determined to try to find another career for Inigo. But his youngest brother had the legendary Velasquez hardheadedness.

"We adore him," Diego said.

"Of course you do. Now, I am going to try to claim a dance with my husband. He's got early surgery tomorrow, so we can't stay late," Bianca said, leaning over to kiss his cheek. Then she gave Pippa a hug before she walked away.

He glanced over at the woman who'd been shutting him down in town but tonight had made the highest bid to spend the evening with him. "You could have saved yourself some money if you'd said yes when I asked you out a few weeks ago."

"Oh, well, then the charity wouldn't have made as much tonight. Somehow, I think that makes it all worth it," she said.

There was something different about her tonight. She was more confident. She'd always seemed to be a little bit on edge, her eyes frequently going to the door of the café where they'd met. It used to bother him when he'd first started running into her in town, but now he'd gotten used to it.

"Was that what brought out your wallet? The charity?"

She flushed again. "It is a very good cause. Children are so vulnerable and really at the mercy of the adults in their lives."

"Were you?" he asked. He couldn't help but be curious about her past. And how could a nanny afford the generous bid she'd placed? Maybe it was because she didn't really have any expenses living in her own house on the Rockin' C ranch. And she'd told him at the coffee shop that her daily lattes were her only indulgence. But still. No one knew much about her. She never mentioned her last name, and he knew from Nathan—Kinley's husband—that Pippa had met Kinley on a bus in Las Vegas, of all places.

But she was a British woman with no apparent connection to her homeland. And Diego, who was proud of being American, didn't understand that.

"I had everything a child could wish for," Pippa said. "The best toys, a first-class education and a stable with horses that even the legendary Diego Velasquez would envy."

"Legendary?" he asked, ignoring the sadness that underpinned her words. So she had been born with money, but when she'd come to the United States, she'd left that behind. He'd seen the way she lived. *Frugal* was one word for it. But it was deliberate.

"Don't let it go to your head, but you are sort of a superstar with horses. I mean, when I've brought Pippa out to your stables to ride, I've seen the way the rowdiest stallion settles down for you."

"I get horses," Diego said.

"But not people?"

"Some people," he admitted. Mo had warned him to not talk about his horses or breeding program around women and bore them when he was in his early twenties. Diego had seen his success with the ladies increase after his brother's advice and still followed it now.

The DJ had gotten set up, and as the drinks from the open bar flowed, more people were moving toward the dance floor. Pippa finished her margarita.

"Do you want another drink?" he asked.

She shrugged. "I'm not a huge fan of tequila."

"What would you prefer?" he asked.

"Something sparkling. I want to celebrate."

He raised one eyebrow and took the margarita glass from her. "I'll be right back."

He went to get them both some prosecco and then returned. "How's that?"

"Much better," she said, lifting her glass toward his.

"What are we celebrating?" he asked.

"My birthday," she said. "I'm twenty-five today."

"Happy birthday, Pippa."

Twenty-five. She was five years younger than him, but the way she said it made him realize there was a lot more to the story. She took a sip of her drink and he did the same, making small talk until they had finished. The band was playing "Despacito" and Pippa was swaying to the music.

"So, Pippa, what are we going to do?"

She tipped her head to the side. "I'm not sure what you mean. What are we going to do about what?"

"This night," he said. He put his hand on her waist and drew her closer to him.

"I'm not sure," she said softly.

Her breath smelled sweet like the prosecco, and her face was so close that his lips tingled. He remembered how soft and succulent they had been beneath his earlier.

"Well, I'm yours…for tonight," he said out loud to remind himself that it was only for this night. "Tell me what it is you want me to do."

She tipped her head back and their eyes met. Her lips parted and he felt her hand come to rest on his shoulder. "Show me a good time, cowboy."

# Two

Once the auction was over and the winners collected their bachelors, it was as if all the tension left the room. Pippa felt freer than she'd felt since…well, ever. Her whole life she'd felt the burden of her inheritance and knew that she'd have to make the right choices when she became an adult. Her mother had coached her and told her to take her time. Not to marry young, as she had, because even though she loved her family she felt she'd missed out on so much of life.

Her father was a different story. Having married into the House of Hamilton fortune, he had wanted to do everything to make his own mark on the legacy jewelry company. But instead he'd always come up short. She knew this from a frank discussion two of her cousins had had with her when she'd turned twenty-one. She had been at that odd age where she was both an adult and also not yet allowed to take over her inheritance, which she couldn't do until she was twenty-five. Her father had full power over many things including voting her shares and her position on the board.

"Another prosecco?" Diego asked, interrupting her thoughts.

"Uh, that, or champagne will do. I'm a sucker for anything sparkling," she said. Now that she'd won the man she'd been eyeing around town for the past two years she had to admit that she didn't know what to do with him.

Her life with Kinley and Penny had been quiet and sheltered. She knew all of Dora the Explorer's little friends but really felt awkward with a man. That was sad. She aimed to fix that tonight.

He snagged two champagne glasses from a passing waiter and handed one to her. "To a glittering night."

She clinked her glass to his and then took a sip. She loved the bubbles in champagne and how they felt on her tongue. She closed her eyes and let the sip stay in her mouth awhile before she swallowed. When she opened her eyes, Diego was watching her and the look in his eyes made her feel…well, not awkward anymore.

The DJ was playing a good mix of dance tunes and slower ballads, along with some standards that got the older generations up on the dance floor, but all Pippa could think about was that she was free. After staying hidden so long, and that being the focus of her every day. Hoping she wouldn't be found before she could claim her inheritance…and now that fear was gone. She'd known her father had private detectives searching for her. And she'd been careful to keep the Hamilton-Hoff name hidden. Not that she couldn't trust Kinley, but if she had to lie, that was her responsibility. Lying was her choice and not one she wanted to force her friends into. All she had to do was wait for her claim to be validated and then…her new life would begin.

"So do you dance?" he asked. Diego's voice was low and smooth. She'd spent way too much time thinking about the way he said her name. He lingered on the last vowel as if he liked the way her name sounded on his lips.

"I do, but mostly with Penny, and that little imp pretty much just jumps around and strikes crazy poses. I'm sure you're not going to want to see me do that," she said.

"I wouldn't rule it out, but maybe not in this venue," he said with a wink. "My nephew is a big fan of lying on the floor and spinning around when the music is on."

"Penny does that, too. I'm pretty sure that's a classic toddler move," she said.

"Can't recall it from my own past, but I hope I had a little more style," he said as the music changed and Justin Timberlake's "Can't Stop the Feeling!" came on. "Want to give it a try? See if you can control the urge to jump around and pose?"

She smiled and nodded. "This song is from the *Trolls* movie."

She groaned internally. She didn't even have a kid and yet kid stuff was all she could talk about. She'd turned into an old lady without even realizing it was happening.

"Please pretend you didn't hear that," she said. "Starting right now I'm going to be young and wild Pippa."

"No arguments here," he said, taking her hand and leading her onto the dance floor.

She'd expected him to let go of her hand, but he didn't. Just held her as they swayed to the music. She didn't have a hard time getting into it and remembered the last time she'd danced like this had been years ago when she'd gone to the winter formal at her boarding school before her mom had died and everything had changed.

After a period of grief, the board of the House

of Hamilton had informed her father that he was no longer an official partner and would only be voting Pippa's shares until she came of age at twenty-five. Her relationship with her father changed after that. And when she turned eighteen, he had become obsessed with who she would marry and determined that she should choose a distant cousin of his who was his protégé.

Unexpectedly she felt the sting of tears and she shook her head until she could shove the emotion back down. She twirled away from Diego, who looked as if he were going to ask a question, and continued dancing with her back to him until her emotions were under control.

So much of her journey had been fed by her mom's death, but she was cool now. She was in control and she knew exactly what she was going to do.

The song ended.

"We've had a lot of requests for this song and I think it's about time I played it. 'Save a Horse' by Big & Rich, so, ladies, grab your cowboy and enjoy," he said.

She knew the song well as it was one of her favorites, but until tonight she hadn't had a cowboy of her own. She did now. She took his hand. All around them on the dance floor, there was laughter that soon turned into close embraces and kisses. But Diego just smiled and kept his eyes on hers as she sang and danced with him.

The crazy surge of emotion she'd had earlier changed into something else as she realized just how long it had been since she'd let her hair down and just danced.

At the end of the song, Diego pulled her close and their eyes met moments before he lowered his head and kissed her. Unlike the embrace on stage earlier, this one didn't feel like it was for show.

Diego and Pippa stayed on the dance floor for the next three hours. Some couples disappeared, then came back looking…well, like they'd enjoyed themselves. But Diego remained where he was. He drank champagne, which hadn't escaped Mo's notice. His brother gave him a look and Diego knew he was going to hear about it later. Alejandro was dancing with someone Diego didn't know, but he was pretty damned sure she wasn't his longtime girlfriend. According to the gossips at the coffeehouse, they'd had a fight about Alejandro's inability to commit and she'd dumped him about six weeks ago.

Pippa stuck close to his side and hadn't mentioned the kiss he'd been unable to stop himself from giving her. He knew that it was a bachelor auction, and all in good fun, yet as he'd held her hand and danced her around the floor, he'd wanted to be hers. He'd wanted her to have really claimed him.

"I don't want this night to end," she said as the DJ announced that there was time for only one more song.

"It doesn't have to," he said. "Wait here."

He went to the bar for a bottle of champagne and two plastic flutes before leading Pippa away from the party to one of the patios that overlooked part of the golf course. It was quiet as they moved away from the party.

"One of the things I really love about Texas is how big the sky is," she said, putting her hands on the railing and looking up. There wasn't that much light pollution out here, so the stars were visible.

"Me, too," he admitted. "Where are you from? I mean, you're obviously British."

"Caught that, did ya?" she asked as she turned and leaned back on the railing.

"Yeah, I'm smart that way," he retorted, pouring her a glass of champagne and handing it to her.

He poured another one for himself as she took a sip.

"I was born in Hampshire, but we mainly lived in London except when I was at boarding school," she said.

"I have to admit I have no idea where Hampshire is," he said.

"That's okay. I had no idea where Cole's Hill was until Kinley moved here," Pippa admitted.

"Why did you come with her? Las Vegas is way more exciting than this," he said.

"I had nothing holding me there. My job as Penny's nanny is important to me," she said, taking a sip of her drink. "I made Kinley a promise when Penny was born that I would stay as long as she needed me."

"You were there when Penny was born?" he asked. This was the most she'd told him about herself since they met, and he was curious.

"Yeah. We were on a city bus when Kinley went into labor. I just stayed with her when she was taken to the hospital because she was scared and alone and we'd been chatting before her water broke… I think we both needed a friend in that moment," Pippa said. There was a note in her voice that hinted there might be more to the story, but she shook her head and looked over at him. "We've been friends ever since. What about you? Who's your oldest friend?"

He took a sip of his champagne. It was never going to replace Jack Daniels as his favorite drink, but the taste was growing on him. "If I'm honest, my brothers. Maybe Mauricio, since he's younger than his twin, Alejandro, by several minutes. Inigo is five years younger than me and closer to my sister, Bianca. He's a Formula One driver like Bianca's first husband was."

Why was he telling her all of this? But he knew. He didn't want to make any moves that would send her running away from him again. Even though she'd bid on him tonight, every other time he'd tried to connect with her she'd shut him down. And he didn't want to let this end.

Not now.

Not until… Well, not until he figured out the secrets behind those gray eyes. She always seemed so calm and controlled, but tonight there was a fire and passion in her gaze that he wasn't going to walk away from until he uncovered its source.

"You have such a big family…like the Ca-rutherses. Is that a Texas thing?" she asked.

He had to laugh. "Well, they do say every-thing is bigger here. The families in Cole's Hill certainly are."

"I guess that's true," she said. "I do like this area of Texas. So lush and pretty with the green roll-ing hills. I mean, it's a bit of a stretch, but it does remind me of our country houses in England."

"Country houses?" he asked.

She shrugged. "You know, big old Georgian mansions that have been in one family forever."

"Then why are you here in Texas and not with

your family?" he asked. "Sounds like legacy is important to you."

"It is and it isn't," she said. "This champagne is really good."

He knew she was changing the subject and he was tempted to let her do it. But the moon was full, and she'd claimed him for her own, at least for this night, and that meant he had nothing to lose.

"It is good, but what did you mean about your family legacy?" he asked. "You don't have to tell me, but I want to know everything there is about you, Pippa… I don't even know your last name."

"Do you need to?" she asked.

"If I'm going to kiss you again, I think I might want to know it," he said. "It's only fair. You know mine."

She was nervous to let him know her last name. It was silly. She'd reached out to her cousins and the board of directors to let them know she was very much alive and ready to claim her seat on the board. Yet here in the moonlight standing so close to Diego, she knew that she didn't want to tell him, because if he knew she was the House of Hamilton jewelry heiress it would change the dynamic.

He thought she was a nanny—

"Is it really that hard to trust me?" he asked.

"Yes. I've been keeping my identity secret for so long that I… Sorry, it's not you. It really is me," she said.

"Why are you hiding it?" he asked.

His voice was silky smooth, wrapping around her senses and making it hard to concentrate. "My father has a plan for my future and I want to choose my own path."

"Fair enough," he said. "So you are on the run?"

"Yes."

He came to stand next to her, leaning against the railing so they were facing the river rock exterior of the Five Families Country Club. "Then just be Pippa for tonight. I promise you have nothing to fear from me."

She reached out without really thinking about it, put her hand on his thigh and squeezed. "I know."

But the electric tingle that ran up her arm made her wonder if she was close to getting in over her head. She wanted Diego. That wasn't a surprise. She'd been dodging him in town and trying to limit their contact for that very reason. It was one thing to hook up for a night but something else entirely to start anything with him knowing she was leaving.

And she was going to have to work really hard

to prove herself once she was back in England. She wouldn't have time for anything else.

She groaned.

He turned his head to face her and in those deep brown eyes she saw desire. He quirked one eyebrow at her and she felt the brush of his exhalation against her cheek. He smelled faintly of expensive cologne and the outdoors. She closed her eyes and took a deeper breath. He smelled like everything she wanted. And tonight he was hers.

She had made a few missteps. Talking about herself and her past. She needed to keep those things quiet.

She opened her eyes and he was still staring at her.

Without saying a word she lifted her hand and ran it over the light stubble on his jaw. It abraded the skin of her fingers, but in a pleasant way. She ran her finger back and forth, and he caught his breath as his pupils dilated.

He reached out and touched her face in return, sending chills spreading down her neck and arms. Her breasts felt fuller and she felt the hot pulse of desire between her legs.

She wanted him.

Her lips parted, and he slowly cupped the side of her face with his fingers, rubbing his thumb over her bottom lip. The sensations intensified, spreading through her body in sync with her heartbeat.

She mirrored his gesture. He had a strong-looking mouth, but it was soft to the touch. And his breath when he exhaled was soft and warm. He'd kissed her twice, but both times had been restrained because there'd been so many people around. This time they were wrapped in a cocoon of intimacy with only the moon and stars to witness their closeness.

And that made this feel more real.

It wasn't just that he'd asked her for honesty and she'd changed the subject. It was that he wasn't deterred by her half-truths and evasions. He wanted her, she thought again. Just her.

Pippa.

She didn't need the Hamilton fortune or her family connections for him to see the woman she was and be attracted to her, and that felt…well, like something she'd never expected to find.

He leaned forward and she removed her fingers from his lips, putting her hands on either side of his face. She needed to do this. He'd kissed her before, but she wanted to be the one kissing him.

She needed this for herself and the self-doubt that had driven her from the only world she'd ever known. In a way, kissing Diego was her way of reclaiming the parts of herself she hadn't meant to discard along the way.

Reclaiming her womanhood.

She wasn't the nanny or a runaway or even the key to the Hamilton-Hoff future. She was just Pippa.

"Diego." She whispered just his name as their lips brushed.

He caressed her, his fingers lightly wrapping around the back of her neck, one of them brushing the sensitive spot behind her ear. Her eyes were half-closed as her lips met his, and she felt his power. But it was tempered. He was letting her take what she wanted from him.

She parted her own lips and felt the heat of his mouth against hers as her tongue darted out and she tasted him. Just one little taste of this cowboy on this big Texas night would be enough to satisfy her.

*Not.*

*Oh, my God, definitely not.*

She thrust her tongue deeper into his mouth for a better taste of him. He tipped his head to give her greater access and she leaned in closer, felt her breasts brush against his chest. His hand on her neck was still light, but the pattern with his finger was driving her forward. Increasing that need to have more of him. To taste more of him.

His tongue tangled with hers and she heard him groan. The vibration filled her mouth and she shivered again as another pulse of liquid desire went through her.

She shifted closer, losing her balance against the railing, breaking the kiss. The air felt cold against her lips and she straightened. Her fingers went to her own mouth as she shifted away from him.

Their eyes met.

"I want to take you home with me."

# Three

Diego took her hand in his. His voice was rough and husky, but he couldn't control that. He'd been turned on by her kiss. Just her kiss had gotten him hotter and harder than he'd anticipated. But she'd said she was on the run…something that he'd suspected, along with most of Cole's Hill. And he didn't want her to feel pressured to go home with him.

"I'd like that, too," she said. There was a look in her eyes that made him even harder and he stood, putting the champagne glasses on one of the tables that lined the patio.

He turned back to her and held out his hand.

She licked her lips and closed her eyes for a second. "You taste really good, you know?"

"I think it was you."

She walked toward him, her hips swaying with each step she took, and he groaned deep in his throat. Damn. She was hot, and she knew it. She kept eye contact with him, but he broke it, letting his gaze skim down her body. He didn't care if she saw how much she affected him.

He wasn't going to pretend she didn't have him hotter than a tin roof in July.

"We'll have to do it again and again until we figure it out," she said. Her voice was husky with a note of teasing in it.

"Sounds like my kind of plan," he said. "I have a town house I keep here in the Five Families neighborhood. Will that be okay?"

"Sounds good. I live out at the Caruthers Ranch and I'm pretty sure we don't want to drive all the way out there. I don't really want to wait that long to touch you again, Diego," she said. Her words adding kindling to the fire that was already burning out of control in his body.

"Good," he said, lacing their fingers together and leading her down the patio walkway toward the path around the golf course. "I hope you don't mind walking, but I've had too much to drink to feel safe driving even just through this neighborhood. It's only a ten-minute walk."

"I don't mind walking at all," she said.

He held her hand in his and tried to concentrate on getting back to his place. But her perfume smelled slightly of spring and she kept humming "Save a Horse," distracting him. Filling his mind with images of her naked, on top of him, riding him. He groaned again.

"Are you okay?"

*"Si,"* he said, falling back on Spanish. His family had been in the United States for generations—their original homestead had been a land grant from the Spanish King back in the 1700s—but their family had always been multilingual.

"I know a little bit of Spanish, but it's not the Mexican dialect that a lot of people speak here," she said. "I had a very funny conversation with Isabella about that the other day. She's one of the new hires that Kinley brought in to work in her wedding and event planning office in town."

Diego didn't really care about all that. But he liked the sound of her voice, so he just made a hmming sound and she kept on talking. Finally, he saw the cluster of townhomes and his own front door.

"This way," he said, leading her off the path and across the street to his place. These townhomes were only about five years old and had been built from the same river rock that had been used in the country club. The path leading up to the front door was made of smaller stones but smoothed out so that it was comfortable to walk on.

He reached into his pocket for his keys, which drew his trousers tighter against his groin, and he realized that even walking and talking about nothing for ten minutes had done nothing to cool him down. But that wasn't surprising. Pippa had had him tied in knots for the last few weeks.

"This is it," he said. "Still want to come in? If not, I can arrange for someone to take you home."

"Diego, I want you. I want this. I'm not going to change my mind," she said.

"You've kept me at arm's length for a while now and I know that there has to be a reason. I don't want you to regret this," he said. He never wanted that. This night felt like…well, a dream, and he didn't want anything to ruin it.

She threw her arms around him and hugged him close. "Oh, Diego, I don't deserve you, but I certainly want you."

"Of course you deserve me," he said, lifting her off her feet and lowering his mouth to hers. Her lips tempted him; the entire time she'd been talking, all he'd thought about was kissing her again.

He set her on her feet and led the way to his front door. He unlocked it, pushed it open and beckoned for her to enter first. They stepped into the foyer. He was a pretty traditional guy, so it was decorated with solid dark wood furniture, and the floor tile was a terra-cotta color that reminded him of the mane of his favorite stallion. He tossed his keys in the bowl on the large chest to the left of the entrance and then undid his tie, tossing it on the table, as well. In the round tile-framed mirror he caught Pippa's gaze.

She watched him with the stark, raw need that he recognized in himself. She moved closer, putting her hand on his shoulder and walking her fingers up toward his neck to slowly pull his tuxedo jacket down his arms and off.

Pippa was glad she'd left her heels on because Diego was taller than she'd realized—at least six-one. She reached around him from behind and slowly removed the studs that held his dress shirt together. It had been a long time since she'd been with a man and she wanted to make every moment of this evening last.

"Hold out your hand," she said, her voice huskier than she meant for it to be.

He did as she asked, and she dropped each of the studs into his upturned palm. She watched him in the mirror as her fingers moved down his chest. It was sexier than she thought to see her manicured nails so close to Diego's tanned chest as each tiny strip of his skin was revealed. Finally, she had the shirt undone to his waistband.

She deliberately rubbed her fingers over his erection. His hips jerked back for a moment and then canted forward into her touch. She undid the button that fastened his pants before tugging the tails of his shirt out. It hung open, giving her a few tantalizing glimpses of his rock-hard stomach and the muscles of his chest in the mirror.

"How are you so muscly?" she asked.

He gave a half laugh, half groan sound. "I spend all my day working with horses that I charge a lot of money for other breeders to use as studs."

"So?" she asked.

"I want the entire operation to project strength and prosperity and success. That means I can't look like a schlub when they show up," he said.

"I like it."

She bit her lip to keep from just shoving her hands underneath his clothes and touching him.

*Patience.*

She could do this. She'd spent years waiting to claim her inheritance. By now she should be very good at waiting.

She reached for his free hand and undid the cuff link, dropping it in his palm with the shirt studs. Then he poured them into his other hand, the small studs and cuff link making an almost musical sound as he did so. She smiled.

Then she undid the other cuff link and dropped

it with the other shirt studs. He closed his hand around them and shoved them into his pants pocket. She focused all her attention on Diego's body.

She pulled the sides of his shirt open and he rotated his shoulders, making it easier for her to take it off. His shoulder blade rubbed against her right breast, sending a hot pulse of desire through her.

He tossed his shirt on top of his jacket and she put her hands on his chest. Diego worked outdoors but didn't have a farmer's tan. It was clear to her that he had spent a good amount of time in the Texas sun without his shirt on. She ran her hands down his chest. There was a tattoo in roman-type lettering that curved around a scar right below his ribs. She suspected that the scar was old as she ran her fingers over the ridge of it. She put one hand on his waist and the other on the small of his back as she leaned around to read the tattoo he had on his chest.

*Courage is being scared to death and saddling up anyway.*

"What does this mean to you?" she asked.

"Just a reminder that getting knocked down doesn't mean I need to stay down forever," he said, putting his hand over hers and rubbing it up and down his torso.

There was a thin line of hair that disappeared

into the open waistband of his pants. She traced the line with her finger as she straightened back up, but he stopped her. He took her wrist in his hand and drew her fingers back to his chest.

"I like the way you touch me, Pippa," he said, his voice that low growly sound that sent shivers through her body. Shivers that seemed to pool between her legs.

She wanted him.

It had been a long dry spell for her and she'd done her share of masturbating and fantasizing about men. Diego had figured prominently in those fantasies since she'd moved to Cole's Hill. She figured there was no way he could live up to them. She'd never had a sexual encounter that had. But there was a heat in Diego's eyes that turned her on. Way more than in her daydreams.

"I like touching you," she admitted, pushing her hand into the open fly of his pants and stroking the hard ridge of his erection through the cotton fabric of his boxer briefs.

He groaned and reached for the zipper in the left side of her dress.

He'd done this before. She knew from the talk she'd overheard in the coffee shop after he'd left that he was a player. There were a lot of women who had either dated him or wanted him in their bed.

"I'm lucky I got you tonight," he said.

"I got you," she pointed out.

"Yes, you did," he said, raising both eyebrows at her as he ran his finger down her side, touching her skin as the zipper opened and the fabric parted.

He slipped his hand in and around to her back and drew her toward him, swaying along as he sang a popular Blake Shelton song under his breath. She closed her eyes, wrapping her free arm around his shoulders while keeping her hand on his erection.

He leaned down, his lips brushing the shell of her ear as he whispered, "This is what I was thinking about each time I held you close to me tonight."

"Really?" she asked, opening her eyes and tipping her head back. Their eyes met and that dark chocolate gaze of his held secrets and passion. She wanted it all.

"Yes, ma'am."

She fumbled around the elastic at the top of his boxers and reached inside to touch his naked flesh. "I was thinking about this."

He didn't say anything. His pupils dilated, and he brought his mouth down hard on hers. His tongue thrust deep into her mouth as he lightly drew his fingernail down her back, stopping at the small of her back. He dipped his finger lower, pushing aside the fabric of her thong panties.

An electric pulse of heat went through her as he cupped her butt and lifted her off her feet. She knew he was moving, but hardly paid any attention to it until he put her back down on the floor and lifted his head. They were in the master bedroom. She could tell by the deep, masculine colors and the large king-size bed behind her.

He disappeared for a minute and then was back with a box of condoms that he put on the nightstand. She was glad she hadn't had to bring up protection, that he'd just taken care of it.

"Now, where were we?" he asked, putting his hands gently on either side of her head and tipping it back. Their eyes met again and he brought his mouth down on hers.

And she forgot about everything.

She let her hand fall from his face to his chest. He was warm. She rubbed her fingers over the scar under his tattoo and then down his abdomen. He shifted his hips and his trousers slid down his legs.

"Impressive," she said.

He wriggled his eyebrows at her. "Thanks. I save that move for special occasions."

She couldn't help smiling at the way he said it. Of course, Diego wasn't like any other man she'd had sex with. He was at ease with his body and with her. There was no pressure to get to it and get it over with. She had the feeling that he wanted her to enjoy this night and that he intended to take his time. There was something sexy in his confidence.

His trousers were pooled around his ankles, but his dress boots kept them in place. His erection was a hard ridge straining against his boxer briefs and his lips were slightly swollen from their kisses. She felt that pulsing between her legs again and knew that she'd never seen anything more erotic in her life. He wasn't posing or pretending. He wanted her and he didn't have to put on moves to impress her.

He lifted the hem of her dress up over her thighs and then all the way over her head, tossing it aside. She stood there in just her tiny panties and no bra.

He groaned, and when he reached out to touch her, she noticed his hand shook slightly. Then he was cupping her breasts with both hands, his palms rubbing over her nipples.

He caressed her from her neck down past her waist, lingering over each curve and making her aware of places on her body that she'd never thought about before, like the bottom of her ribs. His fingers dipped between her legs, pushing her panties down her legs until she stepped out of them, placing her hand on his shoulder to keep her balance. He dipped his hand between her legs, rubbing his finger over her clit until she felt her legs go week.

He put his arm around her waist and lowered her back on the bed, coming down over her. She drew her hand down the side of his body, wrapping her hand around him, stroking him from the root to the tip. On each stroke she ran her finger over the head and around to the back of his shaft. He shivered each time she touched him there.

He ran his hands all over her torso, cupping both of her breasts this time. She shifted, keeping her grip on him but moving so that he could touch her the way she liked it.

She pushed her shoulders back and watched as he leaned forward. She felt the warmth of his breath against her skin and then the brush of his tongue. He circled her nipple with it, then closed his mouth over her and suckled her deeply.

She stroked him until she felt his hips lift toward her, moving in counterpoint to her hand. She reached lower and cupped him, rolling the delicate weight of him in her fingers before squeezing slightly. He groaned and pulled his mouth from her breast. He gripped the back of her neck and brought her mouth to his.

As he drew her against him, she didn't move her hand except to guide the tip of his erection to enter her.

He slid a little more into her and she reveled

in the feel of his thick cock at the entrance of her body. But then he lifted his head and took her nipple in his mouth again, biting down lightly on her nipple, and she shuddered.

She tried to impale herself on him, but he wasn't about to let her have him now. He held her where she was with just enough connection to drive both of them mad.

"Are you ready for me?"

"Yessss," she said with a sigh.

A second later he thrust into her, filling her completely.

She rocked her hips, forcing him deeper into her body. He hit her in the right place and she saw stars dancing behind her closed eyelids as he pulled out and thrust back inside her.

He held her with his big hands on her ass, lifting her into each thrust, and soon she was senseless. She could do nothing but feel the power of his body as he moved over her and in her.

She held on to his sides while he continued to drive her higher and harder, and then she felt everything inside clench as her orgasm surged through her. She cried out his name as he tangled one hand in her hair and drove into her even harder and faster, and then she felt him tense and groan as he climaxed. He thrust into her two or three more times before shifting to rest his forehead against hers.

She looked into those dark eyes of his and knew that everything had changed. She had thought this night would be just sex. Just some fun. But Diego wasn't just a fantasy—he was a real, flesh-and-blood man.

He rolled to his side and disposed of the condom before settling back into bed and pulling her into his arms. "Thank you for tonight."

She nodded against his chest, unable to find the words she needed to say. He drifted off to sleep, but she lay there thinking about her future, which was so much more complicated now.

# Four

Pippa stretched and rolled over, slowly opening her eyes. It was Monday morning. Usually Penny had her up before this, but then she remembered she'd stayed over at Diego's. She sat up and looked around the empty room. The house was very quiet and, if she had to guess, empty.

"Crap."

She hadn't meant to stay out all night. She put her hand on her head, thinking of walking back to the country club in her dress from last night while parents were making the school run.

She wasn't embarrassed by what had happened. She had woken up exactly where she wanted to be, but at the same time she had to face those moms and dads when she picked Penny up from preschool this afternoon.

She glanced at the nightstand. It was only seven. So not that late, but still. She saw there was a piece of monogrammed stationery with bold masculine handwriting on it. She reached for the note and rubbed her eyes before she read it.

Good morning,
I had to leave early to do the morning chores on the ranch. We have a mare coming in to be covered later today and I need to get things ready. I'd love to see you for lunch or dinner. Text me when you wake up. I had your car brought to the house and I've laid out some sweats and a T-shirt in the bath-room. Sorry I wasn't here when you woke.
Diego

"What am I going to do?" she asked the empty room as she fell back on the pillows. Diego was her one-night hookup. Her bit of fun before she left Texas and went back to her real life. She could just say no and never see him again. There was nothing stopping her from doing just that.

But she didn't want to.

She grabbed her phone to text Kinley and saw she had two messages. The first was clearly from

Penny. The four-year-old used the text-to-talk feature on Kinley's phone all the time. The message just said Pippy, where are you?

Kinley's message said:

Ignore the scamp's message. I told her you had the morning off. I assume you are with the hot rancher you outbid everyone for last night, I want deets.

*Ugh.*
*Double ugh.*

She tossed her phone on the nightstand without responding, made her way to the bathroom and took a quick shower, avoiding looking at herself in the mirror until she was clean and wearing Diego's sweats. They were huge on her but super comfy. She took a deep breath. If she had a cup of coffee, she'd start to feel human again.

She went downstairs to find her clutch and found a coffee mug next to the Keurig machine. She made herself a cup and then went back up to the master bedroom to gather her stuff. Diego had even laid out a duffel bag and a pair of flip-flops near the foot of the bed. She had to smile. He'd thought of everything.

Which shouldn't really influence her decision to see him again, but it did.

Heck, everything about Diego made her want

to see him again. It would be easy to say that waiting four years to have sex would have made any partner seem…well, better than they might really be… What the hell was she thinking? She could have had sex a week earlier with someone else and Diego would have wiped that from her memory. Her body ached to have him again. She remembered the way he'd felt between her thighs and craved more of him.

But he wanted… Well, it seemed like he wanted to get to know her. And until she reclaimed her inheritance, she really needed to lie low and stay off her father's radar.

In Texas…

It had been the perfect spot for her to hide out until she came of age. But now that the time had come, starting something with Diego, all the while knowing she was leaving in a few weeks… Was that a dick move?

She felt like it might be.

She saw a message flash on her phone and went to pick it up. Kinley again.

At the office, stop by if you are still in town.

Pippa knew Kinley would be brutally honest with her about the situation with Diego. Her friend was just always that way with everyone.

She grabbed the duffel bag, her phone and

Diego's note and went downstairs to collect the rest of her things.

She found the alarm code on a Post-it on the inside of the front door and entered it to let herself out. She walked to her car without glancing at the street and got in, sitting there for a moment before starting the engine.

She drove through town to the bridal shop that Kinley ran as a satellite to her boss Jacs Veerling's Vegas bridal operation. It was through her work that Kinley had first come to Cole's Hill. She'd been sent here to plan former NFL wide receiver Hunter Caruthers's wedding. Of course, she hadn't wanted to come, given that Hunter was her baby-daddy's brother and said baby-daddy had no clue he had a kid. There had been a bit of a rough patch where Nate hadn't realized that Penny was his child, and when he found out, he blew up at Kinley. But after the family drama had died down they realized how much they loved each other and got married.

Pippa groaned as she noticed that all of the pull-in parking spaces were taken and she'd have to parallel park. When she was done about five minutes later, she walked into the bridal showroom. It was an elegant space that had been designed to suggest understated opulence. Classical music played in the background. Pippa knew that she'd take some of the design elements from this small bridal shop with her when she returned to London and claimed her place on the board of House of Hamilton. The royal jewelers needed to attract a younger crowd and Pippa was determined to do that.

She sighed, realizing she already knew the decision she would make regarding seeing Diego again.

It had to be a no.

She wanted the chance to prove herself to her family and the world more than she wanted a new lover.

Diego hadn't expected his younger brother to be waiting when he got home to Arbol Verde, but Mauricio was sitting in the breakfast room enjoying huevos rancheros that had been prepared by Diego's housekeeper, Mona. And he was drinking a Bloody Mary, unless Diego was mistaken.

"No need to ask how your night was," Mo said as Diego entered the room.

"Same. Struck out?"

Mauricio shook his head. "You don't even want to know. Breakfast or shower first?"

"Shower. I assume you're going to still be waiting when I get out," Diego said.

"Yes. It's business. I have a line on a piece of property on the outskirts of town that is exactly what you're looking for," Mauricio said. "Go shower. I'll wait here."

Diego started to turn away, but Mo had that look like he'd been rode hard and put away wet, which wasn't how Diego wanted to see any of his brothers.

He walked over and pulled out one of the ladder-back wooden chairs, spinning it around and straddling it. He reached out and snagged a piece of the maple and brown sugar bacon that Mona always had on the breakfast table.

"What happened last night?"

"Hadley was there," Mauricio said.

Of course she was. "I thought she moved to Houston."

"She did. But she came back for the auction," Mauricio said before he took a long swallow of his Bloody Mary.

"You broke up with her," Diego reminded his brother as gently as he could. Hadley and Mo had been a couple since high school. He'd followed her to the University of Texas, and when they'd come back to Cole's Hill, everyone expected them to marry, including Hadley. After waiting five years—longer than most women would, according to Bianca—Hadley had given Mo an ultimatum and he'd balked.

Hadley had packed up and moved out of the town house they'd shared and started dating again. Since then, if gossip was to be believed, Mauricio had had some wild hookups out at the Bull Pen.

The Bull Pen was a large bar and Texas dance hall on the edge of Cole's Hill. It had a mechanical bull in the back and live bands performed there nightly. It was respectable enough early in the evening, but after midnight things started to get rowdy.

"I know that, D. I didn't mind it when she was flirting with men. I knew she wasn't taking any of them seriously. But she was with Bo Williams. Sure, according to Mom he's one of the most eligible bachelors at last night's charity auction. But that guy isn't right for her. You know he's just using her to get back at me."

Diego knew the guy and understood his brother's anger. The two men had been fierce rivals all of their lives. They'd competed on opposing Pop Warner football teams during their youth, both bringing their teams to the Super Bowl more than once. And the rivalry had continued in middle and high school. But Diego had hoped now that both men were in their midtwenties, it was a thing of the past.

"Possibly."

"Whatever," Mo said. "I thought you'd be on my side."

"On your side? What did you do?"

Mauricio turned his head and mumbled something that Diego hoped he heard wrong.

"I couldn't hear that."

Mauricio stood up. "I told her that guy was just using her to get to me, and then he punched me, so I punched him back—"

"Where did this happen?"

"At the Grand Hotel bar. They walked in while I was there with Everly—just talking. You know, she's Mitch's gal. The evening didn't end well."

Everly was Hadley's sister and probably not a huge fan of Mo. "Ya think? Mo, do you want Hadley back?"

"I don't know," Mauricio said. "But I don't want anyone else to have her, either."

Diego stood up and put his hand on his brother's shoulder. "Dude, I know it's hard, but you can't have it both ways."

"I know that. I just need time," he said. "I told her that."

"Then she's the one with the reins," Diego pointed out as delicately as possible. He knew his brother had to understand deep down; he was a smart, considerate man who really cared for Hadley.

"I'm screwed."

"Why? Move on."

"I can't. It's complicated. If I give in, she'll

know she has me. That I care more for her than she does for me," Mauricio said.

"Love doesn't work that way," Diego told his brother.

"How the hell would you know? You've never been in love," Mauricio pointed out.

"True," Diego said as an image of Pippa spread out underneath him last night danced through his mind. "I just don't think couples should keep score. No one wins in that scenario."

"You're right," Mauricio said. "But I keep doing stupid things and she pushes my buttons, too. I mean, why did she bid on him?"

Diego had no idea. It would be so much better for Mauricio to have this conversation with their sister. Diego almost pulled out his phone to text her but knew that Bianca would want to know what had happened last night with Pippa, and he wasn't ready to talk about that yet. And Bianca wouldn't let it go the way Mo had.

"Women are a mystery. I mean, Pippa has been flat-out turning me down every time I've asked her out for the last three weeks, and then she bids on me last night. How does that make any sense?"

Mauricio shook his head and started laughing. "Damned if I know. I wish women were as easy to read as real estate."

"Never say that to a woman," Diego warned his brother. "I have some new horses coming this morning if you want to hang around and get your hands dirty."

Mauricio nodded and then went back to eating his breakfast. Diego got up, heading toward the hallway, ready for that shower.

"D?"

He glanced over his shoulder at his brother.

"Yeah?" he asked.

"Thanks. I know I'm being an ass where Hadley's concerned, but I can't help it."

"It's okay, Mo. You'll figure out how to let go and then things will be back to normal," Diego said with a confidence he wasn't sure was justified. Where his brother and Hadley were concerned, he doubted that anything would be that simple.

"So spill," Kinley said as she hung up the phone and turned her brown eyes on Pippa.

She flushed. "What exactly are you hoping to hear?"

"Something that will take my mind off Nate," Kinley said, shuffling papers on her desk.

"Uh, you bid on him and then pretended to lasso him on the dance floor before you led him out of the country club," Pippa pointed out with a smile. "Did you get to ride your cowboy? Maybe you should spill."

"Fair enough, but I need some more coffee.

What about you? I assume you didn't stop at the coffee shop dressed like that," Kinley said, giving Pippa the once-over.

"No. I didn't want to get out of the car in Diego's sweats." She felt the heat creeping up her neck. She had no reason to be embarrassed that she'd slept with Diego last night. Yet somehow… she was. She knew it was because she liked him and she also knew she wasn't going to sleep with him again.

It was so complicated.

And she could even argue that she was the one who was making it so.

"Pip?" Kinley asked.

"Mmm-hmm?"

"I asked if you wanted an extra shot of vanilla in your latte this morning," Kinley said.

"Yes. Sorry. I'm trying to figure out Diego and everything and it's…complicated."

She had to come up with another way of describing this thing with him other than just saying it was "complicated." Kinley didn't even know that Pippa was leaving. She hadn't wanted to say anything to anyone—even Kinley—until she was in the clear. Old enough to inherit without any restrictions. She couldn't let a man throw her off course. True, it wasn't like this was the first time a man had thrown a wrench in her plans, but it definitely was different this time.

Diego made her want to stay and let him continue to interrupt her plans, while her father had made her chafe and eventually left her no choice but to run.

"Why? Also, two pumps of vanilla?"

"Yes. Two pumps," Pippa said. Normally she had only one because she liked to watch her sugar intake, but this morning she needed the boost of sugar and caffeine. "I have a lot to tell you."

"I've heard that Diego is a good lover," Kinley said.

"Not that, Kin. He is, but I'm not talking about that right now," she said.

"Why not?"

"I don't know. What do you want to know?" she asked.

Kinley waggled her eyebrows at Pippa as she handed her the coffee mug and then went back to make her own. "Everything. I told you about that hot night I had with Nate when we were on his balcony."

"You did. That was hot. Well, Diego was a very good lover. He likes to wait for my reactions and he made me feel like I was the only woman in the world that he wanted in his bed."

"Sounds perfect. How is that complicated?" Kinley asked, taking her own mug and coming to sit down on the love seat next to Pippa.

She took a deep breath and turned to face the

woman who was closer to her than any blood relative. She hoped that Kinley wouldn't be upset when she told her the truth of her past.

"I— Well— I'm— That is to say—"

"For the love of God, what the heck are you trying to say?" Kinley asked. "Whatever it is, I've got your back, girl. You know that, right?"

"I do know it," Pippa said, hugging Kinley with one arm. "That's what makes this harder to say. You know how I ran away from home and have been hiding since?"

"Yes," Kinley said, hugging her back. "Did they find you? Nate and I will protect you. And Ethan is a damned good lawyer, so he can get involved, too. Just tell us what you need."

"You are the best, Kinley," Pippa said. "I am so lucky I was on that city bus in Vegas when you went into labor."

"I feel the same way. So let me help you out. You've done so much for me," Kinley said. "What's going on?"

"Um, I ran away when I was twenty-one because I had no control over my inheritance or my life. My father was pressuring me to marry a man who he wanted to take my place on the board of our family company."

Kinley arched both eyebrows. "That's interesting. Who are you?"

"Um…well, Pippa is my name. I mean, everyone calls me that, but my given name is Philippa Georgina Hamilton-Hoff. My family owns the House of Hamilton jewelers by royal appointment of the Queen."

"Shit. Are you serious?"

"Yes."

"So what's changed?" Kinley asked.

"I turned twenty-five. That's when my shares in the company and my inheritance becomes mine to control. They are a legacy from my mother. My father had hoped by marrying me to one of his distant cousins that he would be able to bring his family into the business and take it over."

"That's a lot to take in," Kinley said. "You're leaving us, aren't you?"

She nodded. "I'm sorry. But you and Nate and Penny are a family now. You don't need me the way you used to."

"That's so not true. But I want you to have your inheritance and stop running, so I am not going to be mad about this," Kinley said. "How long do we have until you leave?"

"I'm not sure. I contacted my mother's solicitor in London yesterday—"

"Because of your birthday?"

"Yes. I mean, I could have waited, but I've been watching the company and they have a big board meeting at the end of November and I want to be able to vote my shares this time," she said.

"Okay. So has he gotten back to you?" Kinley asked.

"Yes. He has to verify I'm who I say I am," Pippa said. "So I'm still in limbo until I hear back from him."

# Five

Diego resisted the urge to pull his cell out of his pocket and check his nonexistent text messages again. He had work to do to get the ranch ready for the sire that was being brought in later in the day. They had their own prize-winning sires and mares, but he liked to experiment with other lines to see if he could breed stronger horses. Diego, as the eldest son, had always been expected to take over the Velasquez stud farm. He'd worked closely with his father and later their foreman to develop his skills at spotting the signs when a broodmare would be ready for a sire. The signs seemed instinctive to Diego now; he found horses so much easier to read than people.

The fifteen hundred acres in Texas Hill Country had been in the Velasquez family since the late 1700s, and Diego and his father worked hard to maintain the ranch's clear roots in its history. The Arbol Verde operation of today encompassed the former Velasquez Stud and Luna Farm, legendary breeding operations whose decades of prominence ensured their bloodstock's continued influence on the modern thoroughbred. Through Diego's careful stewardship of the land, Arbol Verde had grown in the last ten years.

He loved the ranch that spread out before him as he sat on the back of Esquire, a retired stud who'd sired three champions, including Uptown Girl. He patted the side of Esquire's neck and then tapped him lightly with his heels to send him running over the grass-covered hills toward the barn. Diego had always had a connection to this land and today it was serving to take the edge off while he waited to see if Pippa was going to text him.

He unsaddled Esquire and brushed him before putting him back in his stall. The ranch was busy and he heard the voices of his other grooms. One of them—Pete—asked for everyone to talk more softly when he noticed that Diego had returned.

His phone pinged and he used his teeth to pull his leather work gloves off before reaching into his pocket to retrieve it. He glanced at the locked screen. It was his sister.

*Not Pippa.*

Bianca wanted to bring his nephew out to ride later in the day. And given that he had no other plans—and wasn't about to contact Pippa first and seem to be more into her than she was into him—he texted back to come on out.

When he was finished working, he walked up to his house. He stopped for a minute to look around the land that had been in his family for generations. Originally his ancestors had been part of the royal horse guard of Spain. His father liked to say that they had been born with an innate horse sense. Diego didn't know about that, but he had no problems with his horses. They made sense. They behaved the way that nature intended for them to. Unlike women.

He rubbed the back of his neck. He wouldn't change his life for anything, but there were times when he wanted…well, things that shouldn't be important. The ranch was his life. His focus should be here.

He saw Bianca's BMW sitting in the circle drive and knew he had to push all thoughts of last night from his mind. His sister would jump on any perceived weakness, and while having a conversation with Mauricio had been one thing, talking to Bianca would lead to him admitting more than he wanted to about Pippa.

He entered through the mud room, taking time to shower off the dirt and put on the clothes that he'd left there. He entered his house and heard a song by Alejandro Fernández and Morat playing and smiled. Bianca had lived in Spain during her brief first marriage and brought back some new influences for their family. Alejandro Fernández was hugely popular there.

*"Tio,"* Benito, his four-year-old nephew, called out as he came running down the tiled hallway toward him, his cowboy boot heels making a loud noise with each step.

Diego scooped him up and hugged him. "So, you want to ride this afternoon?"

*"Sí.* I have to practice every day because Penny lives on a ranch now and she rides more than me," Benito said.

"Why does that have anything to do with your riding?" he asked. But he knew his nephew and Penny were best friends.

"I like her," Benito said, as if that was the only explanation needed.

And since he seemed to be developing a crush on a girl who wasn't texting him, Diego got where his nephew was coming from way too well. "You are always welcome to come and ride. In fact, *Tio* Mauricio and I are looking into opening a riding center closer to town. Maybe you and your friend can ride there."

"Is that true?" Bianca asked, coming out into the hallway and joining them.

"Yes. He was here this morning discussing it," Diego said.

"Really? That's odd. I thought I saw your truck parked in front of your town house this morning," Bianca said.

"What were you doing up that early?" he asked. Bianca was five years younger than him, and as the only girl in a family dominated by boys, she'd learned to hold her own. In fact, Diego would rather get in a rowdy fight with all of his brothers than have a one-on-one conversation with Bianca.

"Derek was on call, so I went over to have breakfast with Mama and pick up *changuito*," Bianca said as she ruffled Benito's hair. She'd called him "little monkey."

"I had a bit to drink last night, so I figured I'd sleep in town," Diego said, hoping his sister would let it drop.

"We can talk about P-I-P-P-A later," Bianca said, spelling out the name so that Benito wouldn't know what she'd said.

"That's none of your business," Diego countered.

"As if that's going to stop me from asking," Bianca said.

Benito squirmed down from his arms. "What is P-I-P—"

"Nothing. Let's get you out to the barn and saddled up. Are you riding, too?" he asked his sister.

"Yes. I guess I can't keep spelling things around this little one," she said as they all donned straw cowboy hats and went to the barn.

"What else did he spell back?"

Bianca blushed. "You don't want to know. Derek thought it was funny, but it was embarrassing."

Diego didn't need any further explanation. He guessed it had something to do with sex and just shook his head.

He accompanied his sister and nephew to the stable, where he kept a mare she liked to ride. As Bianca started to groom her, Diego took his nephew out, distracted for the afternoon from his phone.

Kinley had a meeting with a bride who'd come up from Houston. Jacs Veerling was one of the top three bridal and event planners in the world and having Kinley running her operation in Cole's Hill was a coup. Many brides who didn't want to fly to Vegas to see the showroom or talk with Jacs were happy enough to come to Cole's Hill. With its close proximity to Houston it was very convenient.

Pippa was at loose ends while Penny was at

her four-year-old prekindergarten program and Kinley was working. It gave her too much time to think and hit refresh on her email again and again waiting for a response from the House of Hamilton solicitor. Simon Rooney hadn't given her a timeline for when to expect his response, but because she'd kept close tabs on the company over the years, she knew that her twenty-fifth birthday coincided with a couple of crucial board changes. One of them was that her great-uncle Theo was retiring. He had no heirs, and though Pippa had some second and third cousins who were on the board, she was the only direct-line heir to the company.

And their charter expressed that a direct-line heir, male or female, had the first right to the chairmanship. And Pippa had been studying for the role. She knew that if House of Hamilton wanted to stay a top luxury brand they were going to have to be relevant in the modern world. She'd been researching the marketing strategies of brands like Tiffany and had focused on that topic in her online courses, earning a master's degree in business. She'd also taken classes in jewelry design in Vegas and Cole's Hill. She'd worked hard for this and was impatient to claim her rightful place at the company.

Though she hadn't used her real name in a long while, she'd prepared a prospectus that she'd sent to Mr. Rooney along with her birth certificate, passport and details of her identity.

"Okay, that's done," Kinley said from the doorway. She wore a slim-fitting skirt that had a slit on one side ending just above the knee. She also had on a pair of ankle boots and a thin sweater. Though it was September there had been a dip in temperatures that signaled fall was just around the corner. "Any news from jolly old England?"

Pippa had to smile at the way Kinley said it with her fake British accent.

"No. I'm jumpy, so I don't want to head back to the ranch. I hope you don't mind me just hanging out here," she said.

"Of course I don't mind. Tell me more about your family business," she said, then giggled. "I'm sorry, but when I hear family business, I think of the mob, and you are so far from that mafia princess image."

Pippa smiled back at her friend. "I'm not a princess, mafia or otherwise. The House of Hamilton—"

"My God. I still can't believe you're going to inherit that company! They're huge. Jacs is going to die when I tell her we have an in there. She's been trying to get them to allow her to use some of their designs for her wedding tiaras."

"I'm not even sure they are going to acknowledge me," Pippa said.

"They have to, right? I mean, you are the heiress," Kinley said. "I should call Ethan…he's the only lawyer I know. He could help you."

She shook her head. "Not yet. Let me see what I hear back from the family solicitor first. What kind of tiaras does Jacs want?"

Thinking about bringing in a new line of business was a nice distraction. It kept her mind from Diego. And she had to admit her thoughts drifted to him far too often. He'd told her to text him and she was ignoring that instruction. She didn't need another complication in her life, but at the same time, he was already distracting her.

She kept remembering how nice it had felt to sleep in his arms last night. To put her head over his heart as she cuddled at his side and listen to it beating. She'd been alone for a long time. Of course, she had Kinley and Penny, but that was different. Last night, for a few moments, she had almost felt like Diego was hers.

It was tantalizing, but at the same time she wanted to handle her situation with House of Hamilton on her own, and she had to wonder if it was a tiny bit of fear that was driving her to think of him as anything more than just a bachelor auction hookup. Fear of facing off with her father had her imagining what it would be like to stay here and pursue something with Diego.

He was a rancher. He was as much a part of

Cole's Hill as the Grand Hotel, the quaint shops on Main Street or the mercantile. He belonged here and he would never be able to leave. And after watching her father and mother, and the manipulation and struggle for power between the two of them, Pippa knew she was afraid to ever let herself commit to a man who would try to control her the way her father had.

And Diego was safe that way.

He was never going to leave Texas.

"What are you thinking about?" Kinley asked. "You have the oddest look on your face."

"Diego."

"Ah. Are you going to text him?" Kinley asked. "I think you should. Why not enjoy your time left in Cole's Hill until you hear back from the lawyer?"

"Because I like him."

"That stinks. I swear if I didn't love Nate, life would be so much easier," Kinley said, then shook her head. "I'm joking. Having Nate makes life so much richer."

She wanted that, yet at the same time it scared her. Then again, it wasn't as if she had a kid with Diego, so she and Kinley were looking at relationships through different lenses. But a part of her wondered what it would be like to have a man who she could be herself with. She quickly shut down those thoughts. Of course, that man couldn't be Diego, because his life was here and she'd told him only half-truths about herself.

Facing the prospect of dinner alone and plagued by the constant temptation to text Pippa, Diego told the housekeeper to take the night off and texted his brothers and Derek to see if anyone was available to head to the Bull Pen. He got two yeses. Mauricio couldn't make it; he was on his way to Dallas to meet with someone who had a portfolio that included some high-end property in the Cole's Hill area. He wanted a chance to be the agent on the listing. Inigo was due to head back to his team for the next stop on the Formula One tour, so tonight would be their last night together.

Diego needed to blow off steam. He pulled up in his Ferrari and got out just as Derek Caruthers pulled up. He waved at his brother-in-law. Derek looked tired—Bianca had mentioned that he'd had an early surgery this morning, which explained why.

"Thanks for the invite," Derek said. "I think Hunter and one of his former NFL buddies are going to join, too. The women are having a girls' night—did you know?"

Of course they were. He could even stretch his imagination and pretend that was why Pippa hadn't texted him back, but he knew when he was getting the brush-off. He'd done it enough times himself.

Yeah, karma was a bitch.

He'd known that forever, but he'd never expected to be on this end of it. Plus, he was nice to the women he slept with and for the most part always called when he said he would. Why would karma be coming for him?

To be fair, Pippa had never said she wanted more than last night. More than what she'd bid on.

"Nah, I didn't know. It's Inigo's last night in Cole's Hill for a while, and I thought we should give him a proper send-off. It's time for some payback for when he put me on a plane in Madrid with a massive hangover the last time I was there."

Derek clapped him on the back. "That's little brothers for you. I'm happy to do my part. It's been a long day for me."

"Bianca mentioned you had early surgery," Diego said. It seemed like Derek wanted to talk, but Diego didn't know the right questions to ask. And he knew a lot of things were private thanks to the HIPAA laws.

"Yeah, it was a tough one. Touch and go for a while. I just need to blow off some steam. And your sister is sweet as hell, so I can't let my temper out at home."

"Do you have a temper?" he asked. Derek had

always struck him as calm, maybe a little arrogant, but not someone with a temper.

"I just get short when I'm tired. It's better if I get that out of my system before I go home. I don't want to say anything to Bianca or Benito that would hurt them," he said.

They entered the bar, which had a mechanical bull in the back and was frequented by the astronauts and technicians from the nearby Mick Tanner Training Facility. The joint NASA and SpaceNow project was focused on training and preparing candidates for long-term missions to build a space station halfway between Earth and Mars. When they did come into town, they tended to get rowdy.

"I'm the same way, but it's just me, the horses and my housekeeper," Diego said.

"You need a woman, Diego," Derek said.

He had a woman. Or at least there was one specific one he wanted, and she hadn't texted him all day.

"I'm good. I like being a bachelor."

"Every guy says that when he's single, but the truth is we are all just waiting to be claimed," Derek said as they found a large high-top table in one of the corners.

"I can see I got here just in time," Inigo said, coming over to join them. "Don't let a Caruthers talk you into monogamy. They are all chained now and won't be happy until every guy in Cole's Hill is, too."

"I'm going to tell Bi you said I was chained to her," Derek said.

"Uh, I'm going to deny it, and I'm her baby brother, so she'll probably believe me," Inigo said with a grin. "Beer or whiskey, boys?"

"Beer for me," Derek said.

"Same," Diego said. It was always better to start slow when he was drinking with Inigo.

When Inigo turned and walked to the bar, Derek took a seat and said, "That one is trouble."

"He is. He's always been wild, and then something happened when Jose died," Diego said. "He's more out of control than he was before. Like he's trying to prove something to someone."

"Bi is worried about him, too. She wants him to stop driving, but there's no way that's going to happen," Derek said. "He's third in the point rankings, right behind his teammate and rival. He wants to beat Lewis. He's not going to stop until he does."

"One thing about the Velasquez boys is we are stubborn," Diego said.

"It didn't skip Bianca as much as she might want to think it did," Derek said. "And I'll deny I said that if you mention it to her."

Diego just shook his head. He felt something that could be a pang in his heart but wrote it off as heartburn from his late lunch. He didn't want to admit that he wanted what Bianca and Derek had. He was happy with his life. A woman wasn't a necessity for him.

But that didn't mean that he didn't wish that he was going home to Pippa tonight.

# Six

Kinley was at her book club with Bianca and the other Caruthers wives. She'd kindly invited Pippa to join, but Pippa had declined. She wasn't sure she was ready to come face-to-face with Diego's sister. Not because Bianca was anything but kind; it had more to do with her own insecurities. She was trying damned hard to convince herself she wanted nothing to do with the long, tall Texan, but in reality she had done nothing but worry about her future, and a chunk of that worry had included him.

So she'd left the Jacs Veerling bridal show-room and driven toward Famous Manu's BBQ to get an early dinner. It had opened less than six months earlier and was a popular spot in town. The owner was retired NFL special teams coach Manu Barrett, who'd bought a second home in the Five Families neighborhood to be closer to his brother Hemi, who was part of the astronaut training program.

Pippa had found that the Southern pork sandwich, without the coleslaw, reminded her of the pork baps she could get back home. She'd placed her to-go order and now sat in the car waiting for her food to be ready, staring at her phone and the text message she'd written, deleted and rewritten a hundred times... Okay, that was a slight exaggeration, but it felt like she'd done it a hundred times.

Sitting in her car in a designer mother-of-the-bride dress made her feel silly. But not as silly as wearing Diego's sweats.

There was a rap on her window and she glanced up to see Diego standing there. *Speak of the devil.* What was he doing here?

"Saw your car and decided to come out and say hello." He was carrying a take-out bag.

"What are you doing here?" she asked.

"The food at the Bull Pen isn't as good as this place, so we walked over to eat, and then my brother noticed your car," he said. She could smell the hoppy scent of beer on him and she realized that Diego had already had more than a few drinks.

"I was going to text you," she said.

"Sure you were," he said.

Feeling defensive, she lifted up her phone so he could see the message she'd just retyped before he'd shown up.

He looked at it and then back to her. "So you weren't lying."

Not about this, she thought. Because now that she'd reached out to her family back in the UK, she probably should talk to Diego about who she really was.

"No. I just… I wasn't sure if you were being nice and I'm not sure if I'm staying in Texas and last night was perfect and I didn't want anything to ruin that," she said in a rush of words. *There.* She'd finally admitted out loud what had been dancing around in her brain for most of the day.

"Perfect?" he asked, leaning against her car. "I think I could do better."

She shook her head. "I doubt it."

"Challenge accepted."

"I'm not talking about sex," she said. "Well, not just the sex. The entire evening was like something out of a dream."

"I wasn't just talking about sex, either," he said, leaning into the window. His black Stetson bumped the top of the door and was pushed back on his head. He reached up, impatiently took it off and hit it against his thigh. "I like you, Pippa. I had a lot of time to think about it as I waited for you to get in touch today."

His words were heartfelt and so sincere she knew that she had to be careful with him. She liked him, too, of course, but most of that attraction was purely hormonal. He cut a fine figure of a man with his muscular shoulders and whipcord lean body. He was wearing faded jeans that clung to his thighs. She was intrigued by his strength. She remembered the way he'd lifted her onto the table in the hallway of his condo.

"Me, too," she admitted. "I know you are out with friends, but do you want to go someplace and talk?"

"Yes. Hell, yes. Let me go tell those yahoos I'm not coming back. Where do you want to go?"

"I don't know. I have my own cottage on the Rockin' C, but that's a little far out of town and you aren't in any condition to drive," she said.

"I'm not. I'll ask one of my ranch hands to come pick my Ferrari up in the morning. Dylan is always hot to drive it, so he'll be happy to do it," Diego said.

She nodded. This would be good. They could talk. She could put on her own clothes, and then maybe she could figure out what she wanted from Diego. She hadn't been lying to herself earlier when she acknowledged that she wanted more than sex. But she also knew she was in no position to ask for more than that.

She was leaving. It wasn't like she was going to fall in love with him and give up her heritage. She'd waited too long for this chance.

She got a text that her food was ready. "Let me go pick up my sandwich. Do you want me to order you anything else?"

"Nah, I'm good," he said. "Meet you back here in a few."

He opened her door for her, and when she stepped out of the car, the slim-fitting dress fell around her thighs. She smoothed her hands down her sides, aware that she was way overdressed for barbecue.

"Damn. You keep getting better looking every time I see you," he said.

She shook her head. "I feel stupid in this."

"You shouldn't," he said. "Come on, I'll walk in there with you."

He held open the door to Famous Manu's and then put his hand at the small of her back as they entered the restaurant. People turned to see who was coming in and one woman muttered under her breath, but loud enough for Pippa to hear, "A bit overdressed."

Diego arched one eyebrow at her. "Mandy, be nice."

It was a small thing, but for the first time she felt like a man had her back. She was probably reading way more into it than she should, but it made her feel good deep inside.

They barely spoke on the drive to Pippa's cottage on the Rockin' C. She had the radio turned to Heart FM, which played soft rock music. The buzz he'd had going was starting to fade, but as usual just being in the same vicinity as Pippa was having a pronounced effect on him.

His skin felt too small for him and every breath he took smelled of her perfume and something that reminded him of sex. It was just her scent, but he couldn't smell it and not be turned on. He shifted his legs, making room for his growing erection as she drove. She was a careful driver, going just below the speed limit and signaling way before she got to the turn-in for the Rockin' C. They were about ten miles from the entrance to Arbol Verde, where he lived most of the time.

She pulled to a stop in front of a mason stone cottage that had a rough-hewn wood front porch. The motion-sensor lights came on as they got out of the car. On her front door hung a wreath that as he got closer he could tell had been made out of toy Breyer horses.

She noticed him looking at it as she shifted her bag of barbecue and fumbled for her keys.

He took the food from her so she could unlock the door.

"Penny made it for me for my birthday," she said by way of explanation. "I'm sure you know that she's horse crazy."

"I do know that. Benito was out at my place earlier today getting riding lessons so he can keep up with her," Diego said, but a part of him suspected that his nephew was always going to be chasing after Penny.

"They are too cute together," Pippa admitted. "I missed seeing them today."

"I want to know more about how you came to be a nanny," he said. "Last night you mentioned you were on the run."

She led the way into the small entry hall. There was a tiled mirror and a table with a wooden bowl and a bud vase containing a single gardenia. She threw her keys into the bowl and flipped on a light as she continued into the great room. He saw a set of stairs to the left that led up to a loft. He guessed it was her bedroom.

Immediately an image of her lying naked in the middle of his bed sprang to mind and he shoved it aside. He'd been serious when he said it was more than sex he wanted from Pippa. Now if he could only get his body on board with that.

The far wall was made of river stone and had a fireplace and hearth dead center. There was a rough-hewn mantel that matched the wood on her front porch and a large clock above the fireplace with a swinging pendulum that ticked off the seconds. Two recliners with a side table between them faced the fireplace, and a large leather couch sat opposite an armoire that he suspected housed the television. The great room led to a breakfast nook with a round table and four chairs.

She led the way to the table. "Let me grab some dishes and cutlery and we can eat."

He set the food down next to a white bowl filled with oranges and continued to look around the house. He noticed there was a small office area in the kitchen with a laptop computer and a notepad. Yesterday's date had been circled several times in red on a calendar.

He saw that next to the calendar was an older-looking silver frame that had a distinctive patina. As he moved closer, he noticed it contained a black-and-white photo of a woman who bore a striking resemblance to Pippa, and was holding a little girl who looked just like Pippa, too. They both were smiling.

"That's my mum and me," she said as she moved past him. "My auntie took the photo."

"What happened to make you leave home?" he asked as they sat down. She'd set the table with place mats, cloth napkins and Fiestaware dishes in a turquoise blue. She had also poured them both glasses of water.

It was the fanciest setting he'd ever seen for pulled pork sandwiches, but at the same time it just sort of felt right considering he was with Pippa.

"Um…well, Mum died when I turned fourteen and my father took over the guardianship of me and my inheritance. He had a different idea for my future, including me marrying someone he'd chosen."

"Are you married?" he asked. He'd never thought she might belong to someone else. Then immediately he realized that he didn't think she was the kind of woman to sleep with one man when married to another. He knew it had been his own insecurity at realizing how much he didn't know about her that had prompted the question.

"No. Obviously not, given what you and I have been up to. I ran away the night he was going to propose," she said.

Diego leaned back in the chair, feeling like a fool as he watched her carefully. She hadn't been kidding when she'd mentioned that it was complicated. He couldn't imagine his father ever trying to control him. If he had, Diego would have done something similar to what Pippa had.

"I'm sorry for asking that. I knew you weren't married. It's just a shock to hear all of this… I mean, I knew you were more than a nanny, but this is bigger than just inheriting some jewelry, isn't it?"

"Yes, it is."

"So what's next? Can you return to England?"

"I have started the process," she admitted. "But they have to verify that I am who I say I am first."

"Is there some doubt?"

"Not really, but there will be questions, and my coming back will make things awkward for my father, who has been managing my assets while I've been missing," she admitted.

"I take it you two don't get along," Diego said. "Stating the obvious, right?"

Her relationship with her father was complicated. Over the last four years she'd spent a lot of time waking in the middle of the night and thinking about how much she hated him. Especially when Kinley was having a hard time making ends meet when she'd first started working for Jacs. If she weren't having difficulties with her father, Pippa knew if she'd walked into the bank and made a withdrawal she could take care of Kin's finances and let her give Penny the financial stake they needed to make a good life.

But at the same time, she'd be giving up her freedom.

Because her father had final say in practically

everything she did with her money and her time until she turned twenty-five. And he got to vote her shares on the board as he saw fit. The only recourse she'd have had was to lodge an objection, which was virtually the same as having no power.

But she also remembered how broken he'd been after her mum had died. How the two of them had sat in their home mourning her. She knew that part of the reason why he had wanted to control so much of Pippa's life was due to losing her mum. But she hadn't been able to understand why his grief had taken this particular form: to control Pippa.

And time had brought her no closer to understanding him.

"I can't say if we got along or not. I had a typical loving child's view of my father before my mum died. But then when I turned twenty-one he gave me an ultimatum, which was the wrong thing to do. I mean, I know I look all sweet, but I'm really very stubborn," she said.

"*Sweet* isn't the first word I'd use to describe you," Diego said. "I've seen signs of that stubborn streak."

She arched one eyebrow at him. She wasn't going to ask what word he would use. Really, she wasn't. "When have you seen me stubborn?"

"When I paid for your coffee and you insisted

on paying me back," he said. "You didn't want to owe me anything."

"Oh, that… Well, I didn't want to lead you on," she said at last.

"By letting me buy you coffee?" he asked. The amusement in his voice invited her to have a laugh at the situation, but she couldn't.

"Yes. I have been waiting to turn twenty-five since the moment I walked away from my old life and I didn't want to give you any encouragement that we could have anything other than—" She broke off, realizing she had admitted to him that she only wanted sex. That hooking up was fine, but anything deeper scared her.

Of course it did. But she hadn't meant to say it as bluntly as she had. "I didn't mean that."

"You did," he said. "Let's be honest with each other, okay? I'm not going to lie. I do want to do more than just burn up the sheets with you. So if we are going to have any chance of making this work, I think we have to both be honest with each other."

She nodded.

*Honest.*

She could do that.

She thought she could. She wasn't lying to him. She'd told him the truth.

"Fair enough."

"So where does that leave us?" he asked after a few long moments.

She stood up and started to clean the table. Diego helped her out. He rinsed the dishes and put them into the dishwasher without saying anything. She suspected he was giving her time to figure out what she wanted to say.

But like the text message she'd struggled to send earlier, she was still confused when it came to him.

"I'm waiting to hear back from my family attorney," she said, using the American term. "I can't do anything, make any real plans until then. Even my money is tied up until my identity is confirmed. So I'm planning to continue to help out with Penny and live here until that's sorted."

Diego wiped his hands on the dish towel and leaned against her kitchen counter. She tried to concentrate on what he was saying, but his voice was a deep rumble that reminded her of last night when she'd lain on his chest and he'd said goodnight to her. The sound had rumbled under her ear.

She knew that she wanted Diego. Wanted to somehow figure out a way to have him and her inheritance. Like one of the fairy tales she read to Penny before bedtime, she wanted a happy ending of her own.

But she'd never been good at trusting others. If

she had been, maybe she wouldn't have run away in the first place. Because she could admit that when she'd first come to the States, it was her temper and her stubbornness that had driven her from the upscale Manhattan hotel to the bus station with only a haute couture dress on her back and the cash in her wallet.

She could have tried to speak to her potential fiancé, but she hadn't known if she could trust him. She'd just felt like everything was out of control.

But in this kitchen with Diego watching her as if she were in charge, she realized she was exactly where she wanted to be.

"Pippa?"

"Hmm?"

"I asked how long you thought you had until they confirmed everything," he said.

"I would imagine a few weeks."

He uncrossed his arms and straightened to walk over to her, his boot heels clacking on the hardwood floor. He stopped when only an inch of space separated them, and she felt the brush of his breath as he exhaled on a sigh.

"As I see it we have two options," he said.

"They are?"

"I walk out of here and we continue the way we had been before last night, smiling politely when we see each other in town but otherwise pretending that there isn't a red-hot spark between us."

She nodded, nibbling on her bottom lip because it tingled when he stood this close.

"And option two?"

"We enjoy the time you have left in Texas together."

"I'd like that. However, tonight isn't good for me," she said. "I have to be over at the big house when Penny wakes up in the morning."

"I crashed your evening, and I'm glad that you allowed me to."

"I'm glad you did. I was feeling…unsure and I didn't like it. I've kind of stayed away from men for the last few years and I feel really awkward around you," she admitted. He seemed so confident, so sure, that she wished she was…well, stronger.

"You're perfect. Everyone says I'm better around horses than women."

"Who says that?"

"My brother, but he has been known to be an ass," Diego said, standing up and walking toward the door.

She followed him, not really wanting him to go but knowing she had responsibilities toward Penny and if he stayed she'd be distracted.

"Good night," he said, picking up his hat and settling it on his head.

"Good night." She reached out and touched his jaw before he turned and left.

# Seven

"Mama said you're leaving," Penny said while she was taking her bath the next evening. Pippa had already washed the little girl's hair and was cleaning up the bathroom while Penny played in the water.

"I am, imp. You know my home isn't here in Texas."

"But I'm here," she said. "And Mama is, too."

She turned to look at Penny, whose red hair, so like Kinley's, clung to her heart-shaped face. There was sadness in her wide, blue-green eyes. The little girl was hurt that she was leaving.

"Nothing is going to change between us,

Penny. I'm still going to be your Pippy and we'll talk every day on the video chat, like Benito does when his mommy is out of town," she said. "You have a daddy now and I think as you and your mama settle here in Cole's Hill, you are going to find you miss me less and less."

Water sluiced down Penny's little body as she leaned over to hug Pippa tight. Pippa wrapped her arms around her.

"I'll miss you."

"I'm going to miss you, too," Pippa said, feeling tears in her eyes. She'd been with this little girl since she'd been born. The bond they had was deep and important. "We'll always be the P girls."

"That's right," Penny said.

Pippa took the hooded towel from the heated rack and helped Penny dry off. Penny fastened the Velcro that made the towel into a sort of robe, put her hood on and ran into the bedroom to get dressed in the pajamas that Pippa had laid out earlier.

She pulled the plug on the bath water and finished cleaning up the bathroom, thinking of how much she'd liked the simple life. But a part of her knew that something had always been missing.

Kinley came in and they read Penny her bedtime story before tucking the little girl into bed.

"Glass of wine?" Kinley asked Pippa as she closed the door to Penny's room.

"Yes. I'm on edge waiting to hear back from London," Penny admitted when they were both sitting down in front of the gas fireplace.

"I'd be going nuts. You know how I am," Kinley said.

"I do. Penny asked me about leaving," Pippa said.

"Yeah, sorry I didn't give you a heads-up. It kind of came out and I decided I should probably tell her the truth," Kinley said. "But I should have had your back and told you first."

"It's okay. I hope that this doesn't change our relationship," Pippa said.

"I'm not going to let it. You know me better than just about anyone and you and Penny have a bond. You're like her best auntie," Kinley said. "You're not getting rid of us that easily."

"I'm glad to hear that," Pippa said. "I have really loved living with you both, but I think it's time for me to claim my life."

They talked about the different couples who had emerged from the charity auction Sunday night. And how sweet Ethan and Crissanne had been when he proposed. Pippa had had a good view of Mason, Crissanne's former boyfriend and Ethan's best friend, as it had happened. And he had seemed happy for the couple, despite the complicated circumstances that had brought them together.

"So what's going on with you and Diego?" Kinley asked in that blunt way of hers.

"Uh, we decided to date while I'm still here," she said. "I told him that I'm waiting to hear from the solicitor in England. I didn't want to lead him on."

"Good idea. So what does dating look like?"

"I'm not sure. He's busy with the ranch and I have Penny, so finding time to get together won't be easy," Pippa said, recalling how they'd been texting most of the day. But she didn't respond to texts while she was nannying, wanting to make sure Penny had her attention.

"Men are complicated," Kinley said.

"But worth the hassle," Nate said as he walked into the living room and gave Kinley a look so hot that even Pippa could feel the heat. She excused herself and walked the short distance to her cottage.

She let herself in and stood in the hallway with the lights off for a long minute. The house smelled of new wood flooring and lemon-scented cleaner, since Kinley had insisted that the housekeeping staff also clean her place. She'd decorated the rooms with some knickknacks she'd collected in town and while she'd been in Las Vegas. There was a small laundry/mud room off the kitchen and a den that Pippa would have made into a library if she were staying.

There were bookshelves on all the walls and a nice window seat that overlooked the Rockin' C pastures. The shelves weren't full, as Pippa's book collection was mainly digital, but she'd recently joined a book club, so one shelf had ten books on it.

She had obsessively checked her email all night long, so she limited herself to one last look at the smartphone that Kinley had given her but kept in Kinley's name, hoping the solicitor had gotten back to her even though she knew that with the six-hour time difference that wasn't going to happen.

Tomorrow was Wednesday. Realistically she knew it was going to take a few days to verify everything, but honestly it felt like this was taking way longer than the last four years had.

Her phone pinged as she was washing her face and she fumbled for her face towel before running into the other room to see who it was.

It was a text from Diego.

A little thrill went through her.

Instead of meeting for coffee in town tomorrow, would you like a tour of Arbol Verde and a late breakfast with me?

Pippa's reply was instant.

I'd love that. I have to take Penny to school so I could be there around nine.

Perfect. Are you afraid of heights?

No. Why?

Just asking. What are you doing now?

Getting ready for bed.

Wish I was there with you.

*Me, too.* She thought it but didn't text it. She wanted to keep it light and casual. Those were her key words for Diego.

What are you doing?

Fantasizing about being in your bedroom. What does it look like? I didn't get a chance to see it when I was there earlier.

*Light and casual.*
*Yeah, right.*
She hesitated for one more second and then tapped out the message she'd been wanting to send since she'd seen it was his name showing up on her phone.

Come over and see for yourself...

There was no response at first, then the three dancing dots that indicated he was typing.

On my way.

Diego had intended... Well, he didn't know what he'd intended. With Pippa he was like a horny guy who'd never been laid before. He thought about her whenever she wasn't with him, wanting her in his bed. Not living on Nate Caruthers's property. Which made him slow down for a second as he was driving his Bronco hell-bent-for-leather down the old country road that connected his property to the Rockin' C.

He drove past the big house and the bunkhouse to the smaller residences behind them. He knew from past visits that the largest of the three belonged to Marcus Quentin, Kinley's dad, the former ranch foreman who'd retired a few years back. The next one was dark and looked empty and the last one was Pippa's. As his headlights illuminated the house, he saw that she was sitting on the porch swing waiting for him.

He turned off the truck engine and sat there for a long minute in the cab of his truck parked in front of her cottage. If she'd changed her mind, he'd walk away.

And actually now that he saw her, that lust-driven rush that had made him hurry over to her was starting to calm. Once he was with her, he could take his time. It was only when they were apart that there was a problem.

Because he knew they didn't have much time before she'd be out of his life for good.

He put his head on the steering wheel.

What was he doing?

This was like Mauricio following Hadley when she was on a date with someone else, wasn't it? Of course, Diego wasn't going to start a fight with anyone, but the situation with Pippa was similarly an exercise in futility. He wanted more than Pippa was ever going to give…or at least that gnawing emptiness in the pit of his soul made him think he did.

He looked up and noticed how she kept rocking on the porch swing. Just sitting there waiting to see what he was going to do.

And he realized she was just as unsure about this as he was. The connection between the two of them shouldn't be this strong. They were supposed to be a bit of fun for each other, casually hooking up and then going back to their real lives.

Except that wasn't what was happening.

Not for either one of them, unless he missed his guess.

He got out of his truck and pocketed his keys

as he walked up the stone path that led to her front porch.

"Hello, Pippa," he said.

"Diego," she said.

He couldn't help noticing she wore a cotton dress that ended at her knees and had a tie front that was undone, drawing his eyes to the hint of cleavage underneath it. She sat there on the swing as if she wasn't sure what to do now that he was here.

"So…still want me here?" he asked.

She nodded. "Yes."

He didn't say anything else, just climbed up the two steps that led to her porch and then went over to stand against the railing. She'd pulled her hair up into a ponytail and wasn't wearing any makeup, but he'd never seen her look more beautiful. It was as if each time he saw her he noticed once again how pretty she was.

"Tell me more about what is waiting for you when you go back to England," he said. It was the subject he was pretty sure was on both of their minds and he wanted to know the details…though he had no idea why. He wasn't going to leave Cole's Hill. His life and his soul were here. The land and his horses were so much a part of the man he was, he couldn't go with her. But he wanted to know what it was that she'd left behind.

She tipped her head back, looking away from him.

"The family business," she said. "My dad and I were never close, and when my mom died, the rift between us widened. He had control of my shares in the business and my other interests until I was twenty-five."

"Okay, so you're twenty-five and going back means you get to be in charge?" he asked, trying to figure out what was at stake.

"Yes," she said. "When I left, he was pressuring me to marry a man who sided with him when it came to the family business and that wasn't the vision I had for it. Obviously, he wasn't going to force me to marry, but I realized he was never going to listen to me. And if I disappeared, it would tie up my shares. He wouldn't be able to vote them until they ascertained what had happened to me. My shares haven't been in play while I was gone and the company has only been able to continue operating as it had been when my shares were last voted. So I was able to slow down his agenda and give myself some breathing room."

He moved over and sat down on the swing next to her, stretching his arm out on the back. She shifted until she was sitting in the curve of his body.

She put her head on his shoulder and then looked at him with those gray eyes of hers, so sincere and full of vulnerability that he wanted to wrap her in a big bear hug and promise she wasn't going to be hurt again. But he knew that wasn't a vow he could keep. The man who'd hurt her was probably going to fight tooth and nail to keep from relinquishing his control over her fortune.

"What can I do?" he asked.

"Just help me forget what is waiting for me," she said. "I like being with you, Diego, because you are so far removed from that world and… don't laugh…but you make me feel as though you like me for me. All the things that aren't perfect don't seem to matter when I'm with you."

"You are perfect, so I don't know what you're talking about," he said, slipping his arm under her thighs and lifting her onto his lap.

Pippa was talking too much. She'd meant to keep most of the past to herself, but there was something about Diego and the quiet confidence in his eyes that made her feel like everything was safe with him.

Her cottage faced the open pasture and the big Texas night sky. The bunkhouse, barn and main ranch building were in the other direction as was the home shared by Ma and Pa Caruthers. It almost seemed as if they were the only two people on the land tonight.

He settled her on his lap and she wrapped her arm around his shoulders. Their eyes met. His were so big and dark with only the porch lights illuminating them. She suddenly didn't know if her trust was misplaced. There was something in his eyes—a hunger—that made him almost... almost a different guy than the one who'd been sweetly listening to her.

There was something almost untamed about him. As much as her mind might warn her to step back from him, there was another more primal part that wanted to claim him. But she'd never be able to tame him because she wasn't going to have enough time to do that.

She shifted so that she was straddling him, and pressed her lips to his. He spread his thighs underneath her hips, forcing her legs farther apart. She rocked back and forth, feeling his erection against her as their kiss grew more intense.

His breath was warm and sweet and smelled of peppermint and whiskey. She pulled back, putting her hands on either side of his face. "Did you pop a mint in for me?"

He flushed, and that charmed her. "Yeah."

"Thank you," she said. "I didn't do anything to prepare for your visit."

"You don't have to," he said. She felt his hands on the backs of her thighs, rubbing up and down and coming closer to her butt with each stroke. He was moving his hands in a counter-rhythm to her hips.

With his big, hot hands on her thighs and his

thick erection underneath her, she let her head fall back as she rode him. She felt the brush of his breath against her neck a moment before his mouth was on it. He kissed her softly at first, but then as his hands urged her to move faster against him, he suckled her neck and shivers spread down her body as she continued rocking against him.

Diego wore a Western shirt that had snap closures; she tugged lightly and they all came undone. She pushed the shirt open before shifting slightly back on his thighs. He eased his legs farther apart and she undid the snap that held his jeans closed and lowered the zipper to see the ridge of his erection hard against the cotton of his boxer briefs.

He shifted again, freeing himself.

He handed her a condom and she smiled as she held it in one hand while circling his nipple with her fingernail, scraping the line where it met the smooth skin of his chest. Then she scraped her nail down his rock-hard stomach, lingering to trace his tattoo before moving lower.

She took the condom out of the package and rolled it onto his length.

He sat up straighter, pulling her more fully into his arms until she felt the tip of his erection against her center. He groaned deep in his throat.

He undid the laces on the front of her dress even farther until her breasts were visible. She hadn't put a bra on tonight, so when he dipped his fingers under the dress fabric, he brushed over her nipple, which made her shiver and rotate her shoulders to thrust her chest forward.

She moved again on his lap, and his hard-on nudged at her center. She loved the feel of his big hands as he put them under her skirt, caressing her thighs and then cupping her butt. He kissed her neck, biting at her collarbone as she shifted so that the tips of her breasts rubbed over his chest.

She shuddered, clutching at his shoulders, grinding her body harder against him.

He moved his fingers lower on her body, until she felt the tip of one tracing her folds and pushing up into her. She was moist and ready for him and leaned forward to take his mouth with hers. He continued to trace the opening of her body with his finger.

She captured his face, tipped his head back and kissed him hard. Her tongue thrusting into his mouth as he shifted, she felt him inside her. She rocked down hard on him as he plunged into her.

He used his thumb to find her center and stroked her as she rocked against him. His free hand cupped her butt and urged her to a faster rhythm, guiding her motions against him. He bent his head. His tongue stroked her nipple, and then he suckled her.

Everything in her body clenched. She clutched

at his shoulders, rubbing harder and tightening around his fingers as her climax shattered her. She collapsed against his chest and he held her close. She put her head on his shoulder and they stayed like that without saying a word.

Pippa wanted to pretend it was because there was nothing to say, but she knew it was because there was too much.

# Eight

There were a lot of cute boutiques in the historic area of Cole's Hill, but Penny and Benito wanted to go to Jump!, an indoor soft play area out on FM145. Pippa had volunteered to pick them up after pre-K and take them to play and then pick out their Halloween costumes.

Bianca had flown to New York to do a one-off fashion shoot for a famous American designer. Rumor around town was that she had been asked to do his spring show but had declined. Kinley was working longer hours than normal and had gone to Vegas with several of her brides-to-be. So Pippa was having both of the four-year-olds for a sleepover that evening. Diego had suggested they go for a ride at sunset and then have dinner around a campfire on his property.

And after securing the permission of all the parents, she had accepted. They had fallen into a relationship that felt…well, like pretend, if Pippa was honest. They saw each other when their schedules allowed and had been sleeping over at each other's places at least three times a week.

She had a feeling in the pit of her stomach it wouldn't last…probably because she knew it wouldn't. But it had more to do with the funky peace they shared. It was like they were both on their very best behavior. So what was developing between them felt fake; at least on her side, she was offering a fake version of herself. She wasn't as sweet and nice as Diego seemed to think she was.

Normally she would have given the barista a bit of attitude when she skipped her pump of vanilla in her coffee, but because Diego had been with her this morning she'd just smiled and said that was okay, she was watching her calories.

And she knew that there was no way a successful rancher like Diego would be in town every morning at the coffee shop. That was prime time on a ranch. She knew because that was when Nate and the rest of the population on the Rockin' C were the busiest.

So Diego was faking it, too.

Then there was the other night, when he'd said he'd rather watch a repeat of the *Real Housewives* than the Spurs basketball game, which she knew was a lie. She smiled at the memory of her teasing him and asking him which housewife was his favorite. When he'd gone into the kitchen to get popcorn, she'd switched it over to the Spurs game. She frankly didn't understand a thing that was going on during the basketball game, but seeing the surprise and relief on his face had been worth it.

She realized that some things weren't fake between them—their passion, for one. But in general, she suspected they were being so careful of each other's feelings because they had a nebulous expiration date on their relationship. They both knew that it would end but not exactly when. And neither wanted to spoil their last moments together.

Whenever they would come.

It had been almost ten days and she'd still heard nothing from the solicitor except that he'd received her information and confirmed her identity. As far as her claim to her entire fortune, and the chair on House of Hamilton's board, he was still working on it. He'd paid her a small stipend via wire transfer to the bank in Cole's Hill. So she had some of her own money, even though she didn't need her fortune to live in Cole's Hill.

Room and board were covered by Kinley and she had an Etsy shop where she sold art pieces she made to practice her skills at design. Some of them were pretty good to her mind, others just so-so.

"Pippy, that was so much fun. I hope that I can find the perfect costume," Penny said as she and Benito came out of the soft play area and she was helping them both to put their shoes back on.

"It looked like fun," Pippa said to her. "Did you like it, Benito?"

"Yes, I jumped the highest," he said.

"He did. I tried to beat him, but I couldn't."

"Not everything has to be a competition," she said to the two toddlers.

"We know," they said at the same time.

"What costumes are we looking for today?" she asked as they stepped out of the play area and she took their hands. The costume superstore was across the parking lot, and since it was a sunny, warm day there was no reason for them not to walk to it.

"Cowgirl," Penny said, skipping next to her.

"I'm not surprised, but you know that Halloween is a chance to be something different than who you normally are. And you're a cowgirl now," Pippa said.

"Really?" Benito asked her.

"Yes. What are you going to be?" the little girl said.

"I was going to be a doctor like Daddy." Benito's biological father had been killed when he was six months old. Since Bianca and Derek had married, he called Derek Daddy and referred to his biological father as Papa. "But I might be an astronaut."

"That's a good idea," Pippa said.

When they got inside the store, Penny went straight for the cowgirl costumes, but she kept looking over at a pink princess one, as well. "What's the matter, imp?" Pippa asked.

"Could I be a cowgirl princess?"

"Yes. Or you could just be a princess," Pippa told her, finding the sizes in both costumes for Penny.

"Yay!" Penny said, turning to help Benito.

He decided on the astronaut and then they both wanted every piece of candy near the checkout, but Pippa got them to compromise on a lollipop and a jar of bubbles instead.

"What about you?" Penny asked. "What are you going to be?"

She didn't know if she'd still be in Texas at Halloween. Surely everything would be sorted before then.

"I haven't decided yet."

"I hope all the good ones aren't gone," Penny said.

"I'm sure they won't be," Pippa replied.

Diego was waiting in the barn when Pippa and the kids arrived. Every time they made plans he was aware of the fact that they might be canceled due to Pippa's situation, and it was setting him on edge. Plus, being perfect—or as perfect as he could be—around Pippa was making him short-tempered with his brothers. Mainly just Mauricio, which suited the other man just fine, since he was out of sorts over Hadley being seen around town with another man.

So the Velasquez brothers were spending way too much time in town at the kickboxing studio that a former army captain and his brother had set up. Diego had a few bruises on his ribs and his knuckles ached, since he and Mo preferred bare-knuckled fighting, but it had been worth it.

He smiled easily at Pippa. She wore a pair of faded jeans that made her legs look even longer than he knew they were and a pale pink button-down shirt that made her blond hair and gray eyes stand out. Penny was dressed in a pair of jeans and boots and had a pink cowgirl hat on her head and Benito had boots, jeans and his black cowboy hat on.

He had his ranch hands set up dinner on one of the ridges that was an easy thirty-minute ride from the barn. He had saddled the gentlest horses he had for Benito and Penny. Pippa had told him that she'd ridden as a child and Nate had said that she was a good horsewoman, so he'd given her a spirited mare who he hoped would match her skill.

"*Tio*, I'm going to be an astronaut for Halloween," Benito said as he came skipping over to him.

Diego scooped his nephew up and hugged him close. He had been happy when Bianca had moved back home after Jose's death, so he could watch his nephew growing up.

"Sounds like it should be fun. I met the brother of one of the astronauts at the training center. Maybe I can arrange for you to go and visit him," Diego said, thinking that Manu would probably be able to arrange that.

"Can I go, too?" Penny asked.

"I think Diego will need to make sure that kids are allowed to go out there for a visit first," Pippa said.

"Yes, I will. But one thing I know we can do is go for a ride on the horses right now. Who's ready?"

"Me!" the children both yelled. Benito squirmed to get down out of his uncle's arms. Diego placed the little boy on his feet and he and Penny joined hands and ran toward the barn.

"Sorry, I was promising something I couldn't deliver, wasn't I?"

"You were," Pippa said. "It's probably not that big of a deal, but Penny will go to school tomorrow and tell everyone you are taking them to the space station and it might start something."

"I guess you can tell I'm not around kids a lot," he said.

"I can and I like it. For once, I feel like I know more than you do," she said.

"That's not true," he responded. "You know tons more than I do about a lot of subjects."

"Not horses," she said.

"Nate said you were pretty good. Was he lying to me?"

She shook her head. "I can ride, but I feel weird sitting on a Western saddle. Kinley's been giving me some lessons on weekends when the little imp insists we all go for a ride together."

Diego pulled her to a stop just outside the barn. He could hear the kids talking to the grooms he'd had in waiting to help them with their tack.

"Won't you miss her?" he asked.

She bit her lower lip. "Yes. I'll miss her terribly, but this isn't my life. I know it, and so do Kinley and Nate. They include me in their weekends, but I know they are looking forward to being a family on their own."

Diego put his arm around her and squeezed her. "I can't imagine what that must be like."

But he could. He was dealing with that to a very small extent with Pippa right now. She was his for these few weeks. It had sounded like a great idea when he was horny as hell; when they were naked it always felt right. But now that he realized he could lose her at any minute, that when he planned an evening for the two of them he had to wait all day in suspense hoping she'd still show up, he knew it wasn't.

If it had been only physical attraction between them, things would be easier. Or if Pippa were a snob to people. But she was sweet to everyone, even the barista who never got anyone's order right. He'd lost it with her more than once, but not Pippa. She'd just smiled and put the other woman at ease.

It had made him realize how much he liked her. He was trying to be smart about this and not get in any deeper than he already was, but the only way that was going to happen was if he kept his distance from her and that wasn't in the cards.

He didn't want to waste a single second of the time they'd been given. So he was working longer hours around the times when she was available so he wouldn't have as many regrets when she was gone.

"What are you thinking?" she asked.

"Just how much I'm going to miss you when you leave," he said, then turned and walked into the barn and went to his horse.

He saddled his horse Iago and heard Pippa talking to the kids as they donned their protective helmets and were assisted onto the horses by the grooms. He guessed he hadn't spent long enough in the ring with Mauricio today, because he was out of sorts and he needed to adjust his attitude.

Hopefully the ride would do that.

Pippa knew she'd upset Diego, and she got it. Really, she did. She probably should just leave Cole's Hill now and not prolong the inevitable. It was just that she had nowhere to really go until the solicitor got back to her. Even her passport was out-of-date. But hanging around here, starting something with Diego even though they'd both said it was just temporary, hadn't really been a smart idea.

"Texas is so different from Las Vegas," Pippa said as they rode. The kids were a little ways ahead of them and Diego never took his eyes off the pair.

"It's beautiful, isn't it? I can't imagine living anywhere but here," he said.

And that secret hope that she'd barely even realized she'd been holding on to died. Diego was never going to be a man she could bring with her to her new life. Not that she needed a man by her side, but it would have been nice not to return to England by herself. And Kinley obviously couldn't come with her.

"Stop your horse," Diego called out to the kids. "Do you remember how?"

"Pull back on the reins," Benito said.

"I knew that, too," Penny chimed in.

The two of them expertly stopped their horses and then held the reins loosely in their hands much the same way Diego did. He guided Iago next to the two children and Pippa watched them look over at him with rapt expressions on their faces. She fumbled for her cell phone and snapped a photo of them as Diego was giving them instructions.

She tucked her phone away before joining them, knowing the photo would be one of her most cherished because it would bring her back to the sun on her shoulders and this moment when she realized that Diego meant more to her than she had wanted him to.

After thirty minutes, they got to the spot where they were going to have the campfire dinner. She saw that Diego had gone out of his way for them. He had four chairs set up around the campfire and had torches lit. One of his ranch hands was cook-

ing the meal and there were two others waiting to
take the horses back to the barn. She noticed he
had a four-wheel ATV parked to the side. There
were jackets for the kids and blankets in case the
evening turned cold, but so far the weather was
perfect, with only a slight breeze.

"I made cowboy chili for dinner," Diego said.
"This recipe has been in our family for almost
two hundred years. In the old days they'd make a
batch of this and it was all the hands would have
to eat for a week."

Benito and Penny both went closer to him as he
told them the history of the first Velasquez ances-
tor who'd come over to Texas by order of the King
of Spain and started to carve out a life for himself
and his family. Diego kept Pippa and the children
entertained as they ate the chili, which he'd made
mild enough for the kids to eat. When they were
done, he brought out the makings of s'mores for
dessert, which she'd never had growing up but
had learned to love since being in Texas.

She realized as they ate dinner how much she
would miss Diego and Texas. The stories here
were big legends that fired her imagination, but
more than that she was going to miss Diego. And
it was clear to her that he wouldn't suddenly leave
his ranch and come with her to England. He
couldn't. His history was here. His horses and his
equine breeding program, which had just received

another award according to a couple grooms she'd overheard discussing it, were all here.

He belonged here. As much as she didn't.

"Cowboys and cowgirls used to use the stars to find their way back home," Diego was saying. The kids had their heads tipped up to the sky. They were far enough from town that there was no real light pollution except for the glow of the torches and the fire.

"I'll show you how when we're done eating," Diego said.

"This summer, Daddy is going to take me to a cattle drive," Penny said.

"Really?" Diego asked. "On the Rockin' C?"

"No. Fort something. Do you remember, Pippy?"

"Fort Worth," she said. "Apparently they still drive cattle down the street there twice a day."

"They do. It's one of the oldest traditions in the state. There used to be a cattle market there and everyone would drive their herds up for the sale," Diego said. As he continued talking to the kids about life on the cattle trail, Pippa just sat there and listened to him.

She wondered why he wasn't married. Diego was really good with the kids. They'd moved to sit closer to him, and he had them both cuddled on his lap as he talked. Their eyes met over the kids' heads and her heart beat a little faster. He winked at her and the earlier turmoil she'd felt between them disappeared at least for a few moments.

She closed her eyes and some of the resentment she had been carrying with her since she'd left her old life dissipated. She'd never have been here if not for those events that had driven her to run away.

"In fact, the Five Families of Cole's Hill used to pool their resources and they would journey up to the cattle markets together. Back then there were all kinds of dangers from snakes to outlaws to treacherous river crossings. That bond was what made Cole's Hill what it is today," Diego said.

They finished their food and Pippa cleaned up both kids' faces and hands. Then they piled into the ATV and Diego drove them halfway back to his ranch house, stopping in an especially dark area. "Close your eyes for a few minutes and then I'll show you the star that will point you to home."

Pippa glanced in the back seat of the open-air vehicle to where the kids were buckled into their car seats. When she turned back around, Diego was so close to her, their breaths mingled. And he kissed her. It was hard, passionate and deep but over before it began. "Couldn't resist your lips," he whispered.

"Open your eyes, kiddos, tip your head back and look toward the front of the vehicle. Do you see the star to the left of the moon?"

Both children weren't sure how to tell left from right, so Pippa moved to the back seat and sat between the two of them to help. She glanced up, pretty sure that Diego meant Venus when he talked about the star that would lead them home. A good Texas legend, she thought, just like the man himself.

She carefully pointed to the "star" so Penny and Benito could find it.

"Now you will always be able to find your way back home," she said.

"We all will," Diego added.

She clamored back over the seat and he drove them back to the ranch house.

"Want to come back to Pippa's for our sleep-over?" Benito asked.

"Um…"

"Please," Benito pleaded.

"It would be nice if you joined us," Pippa said.

"Then I will," he said. "I have to be back at the ranch first thing in the morning."

"That's fine," she said.

Pippa got Penny into her car and Diego followed her with Benito. As she drove away, she couldn't help thinking that home wasn't what she'd once believed it would be. For one thing, she hadn't imagined she'd live anywhere but London, but now her idea of home was changing and morphing into something new. And that was dangerous.

# Nine

Diego followed Pippa in his ranch truck with Benito buckled into his car seat beside him. His nephew talked excitedly all the way back to Pippa's cottage.

By the time they got there, the kids were exhausted from their outing. Diego helped Pippa get the kids bathed and into bed and then hung back waiting for her to check her email.

"Nothing firm yet. But I did just get a brief email. The solicitor said he should have news no later than Friday," she said.

*It was Wednesday.*

So that meant he had two more nights with her.

His gut said he needed to take her as many times as he could. Imprint on her so that when she was back in the UK she wouldn't be able to forget him or their time together.

He took her hand. "Can you hear the kids if we're downstairs?"

"Yes. I have a monitor app on the smartphone that Kinley gave me," she said. "Why?"

"I want you," he said, under his breath.

She flushed. "Me, too."

He led her down the stairs after she made sure both kids were sleeping in her big bed, then into the kitchen, where he lifted her up onto the counter and tunneled his fingers into her hair and kissed her deeply.

He had told himself this was so she wouldn't forget him, but he knew this was for him. He wanted her as many times as he could have her and in as many different ways. For himself. For those long winter nights he knew were coming. Long nights when he'd be all alone and hungry and hard for a woman who had never thought of him as anything other than her temporary man.

She pushed her hands up under his shirt and then reached into the back of his jeans, cupping his ass and drawing him farther in between her legs. He shifted around, rubbing the tip of his erection against her. Running his hands up and down her back, he pulled her forward toward him, but there was too much clothing in the way.

His jeans, her jeans. He lifted her off the counter and knelt to help her take off her boots. She put one foot on his thigh. He grabbed the toe with one hand and the heel with the other and helped her take off the first boot. Then he made quick work of the other.

She was wearing socks with hearts and flowers on them. He pulled them off and tossed them toward her boots. Her feet were small and delicate in his big hands. Her pedicure was a racy red color that matched the lipstick he recalled her wearing to the bachelor auction.

His cock jumped as he remembered the way she'd looked that night, and he groaned at the pain. He straightened and reached for the button at his waistband and undid it, lowering the zipper so that his erection had room. She reached down and touched the tip of it, stroking with her fingers in the opening of his jeans.

He took her hand in his and placed it on the counter next to her. He was so close to the edge that if she touched him again, he'd spill himself right there and this would be the shortest encounter in history. And he needed more than that.

He undid her pants, pushing them down her legs along with her panties. As she scissored her legs and the jeans and underwear fell to the floor, he reached into his back pocket where he'd put a condom earlier this evening.

She smiled and took it from him.

"I like a guy who's prepared," she said.

"Just call me a Boy Scout," he said. He was always prepared for sex. But he was also trying to be prepared for when she left. He shook his head, tore open the packet and shoved his underwear down to put the condom on.

She placed her hand on his hip and he realized he was going too fast. The control he'd always taken for granted had deserted him. That email from her lawyer had just served to remind him of how little time he actually had left with her. And that was doing things to his emotions that he didn't want to deal with.

But she was his for now. That was about as much as he wanted to think about tonight. He pulled her toward him.

"Wrap your legs around me," he said. She did as he asked, and he shifted his hips, feeling the tip of his erection nudging at her entrance.

But she wasn't ready, and he cursed. He brought his mouth down on hers and his hands to her shirt, undoing the buttons while his tongue teased and played with hers. She sucked his deeper into her mouth as her hands cupped his backside and she drew him closer. She arched against him as his fingers found the cami bra she had on, and he fumbled around, trying to find a fastening before realizing there wasn't one. He pushed the bottom of the bra up until her breasts were free and then he rubbed his finger around her nipple, feeling it bead under his finger.

She parted her legs farther and he plucked at the nipple as he once again thrust against her. This time he slid easily inside. She arched her back and he looked down at her breasts angled toward him, lowering his head to catch the nipple of one in his mouth and sucking on it hard and deep.

She funneled her fingers through his hair and rocked harder and harder against him until he heard that tiny gasp and knew she was close to her climax. He lifted his head from her breast and took her mouth in an urgent kiss, swallowing her cries as he drove into her again and again until he came long and hard. She tightened around him, her body squeezing him so perfectly, and he kept thrusting until he felt her shiver in the throes of orgasm.

He held her against his chest as their breathing slowed and his heartbeat started to calm. She wrapped her arms and legs around his body and held him tightly to her.

And he hoped he wasn't the only one who was going to have a hard time saying goodbye.

Diego knew he couldn't spend the night, but he didn't want to leave. So instead he convinced

Pippa to take the baby monitor with her to her back porch, where there was a fire pit. He lit a fire and then sat down on one of the big Adirondack chairs, pulling her onto his lap.

"Did you always know that you were going to take over the stud farm?" she asked, leaning her head against his shoulder.

He knew his arms were going to feel empty when she was gone and hugged her tightly to him without saying a word.

"Yes," he said at last. Sparks from the fire danced up into the night sky as a log shifted. He stared at it and pondered their situation.

If he were a different man, he'd just give up everything and follow her, but he wasn't. He'd always just known that he was meant to stay at Arbol Verde. He'd never had a moment of doubt. He'd gone to Texas A&M and studied animal husbandry, coming home on the weekends because he'd missed the land and his horses.

He was trying to find a way to keep seeing Pippa when she returned to the UK, not that she'd even suggested the possibility. But Diego knew that he wasn't going to transition well to living without her. A part of him wondered how he could have such strong feelings for a woman he'd known for such a short time.

But she wasn't just a woman. She was Pippa.

She was classy and funny, feisty and sexy. But

she was still a mystery to him no matter how much they talked and he knew that letting her go was going to be hard.

"Tell me about it," she said, a note of humor in her voice.

What was there to say? "You know how some people grow up and can't break free from their hometown?"

She nodded. "Yes, but I wasn't one of them. I wanted out from under my father's thumb something fierce."

"I didn't have that. My dad and I have always been on the same page when it comes to the stud operation. My earliest memories are of following him around the barn. I think I learned to ride as soon as I could sit in the saddle. There was never a moment when I felt like I didn't belong to the land," he said.

She nodded. "I wish I had that sense of belonging. I've felt lost over the last few years, but at least finding Kinley and helping her to raise Penny grounded me somewhat. I mean, I knew it was temporary, but at the same time I couldn't have wished to be anywhere else. It was the closest I'd come to having a home since my mom died."

"I'm sorry you lost your mother," he said. He didn't ever let himself think what life would be like without his mama. She was a force of nature. With her long career in television, she'd always been outspoken and encouraged her kids to be the same.

"Thanks. I didn't realize what a barrier she was between my father and me until she was gone. Most of the year I was at boarding school, but once she was gone, my father and I hardly saw each other. I had never realized how hollow that relationship was. I thought… Well, it doesn't matter because I was wrong," she said.

She turned to face the fire, leaning forward, and Diego realized that talking about her father made her put a barrier around herself. He doubted she was even aware of it, but she'd just changed. There was a coldness that hadn't been there a moment before.

He wanted to pull her back against him, but he was already holding on too hard and knew that he wouldn't do it. "Tell me about your family business."

"We design high-end jewelry," she said. "I have been taking business courses through an online university while I've been living with Kinley and I did a few extension classes in art."

"Have you made any designs to take back with you?" he asked.

"Yes. I've made a lot of them, but ours is a legacy brand. Part of the falling-out I had with my father was that I wanted us to move with the times, become more modern," she said.

"Will the rest of the board support you?" he asked. "You said he votes your shares, so I assume that all of the board members are family, is that right?"

She pushed herself off his lap, walked a few steps away and stared up at the night sky. He wondered what she was looking for.

She glanced back at him, her long blond hair sliding over her shoulder. "Yes. Most of them are family, but they are second and third cousins... I'm the main shareholder."

"So your father has been controlling the company because of that?" he asked, trying to understand what she was going to be up against when she returned to England.

"Yes. He and my mother were third cousins, so he has a small stake of his own in the company, but voting mother's shares, which are now mine, gives him a majority vote. I think he will fight against me being reinstated."

Diego hoped not. He could see the struggle in Pippa's face as she talked about the company and her father. It would be better if the old man just graciously accepted her return and stepped aside.

"Do you think there is a chance he's mellowed? Perhaps your being missing for all this time has made him realize what he'd lost," Diego said.

"That's a nice thought," she said. "But I doubt very much that's the case."

He wanted to give her space. To be cool and pretend that she hadn't already made him care more than he wanted to. But he got up and went to her, pulled her back into his arms and held her until the fire died and they both went inside. He wanted to stay and claim every second he had with her before she had to leave. But the kids were upstairs. After saying goodbye, he drove home, away from her, wondering what the future held for her and how he was going to manage his part in it.

Penny and Benito were up early and Pippa, who hadn't really slept at all, struggled not to be cranky with them. She was very happy when Kinley, who'd come back from Vegas overnight, had volunteered to take them to school. She passed the children off to her friend, who looked like she wanted to ask questions, but Pippa just shook her head and waved them all off.

She went back to the computer. Still no email about her request to assume her position on the House of Hamilton board and be put in full control of her fortune. She was frustrated and more than a little angry with herself because she knew that a part of her wasn't upset about the lack of progress on that front. The longer it took to hear back from the solicitor, the more time she'd have with Diego.

And what did that say about her?

Hadn't she seen what happened when a man she cared about tried to take control of her life? Wasn't she right now in this mess because her father had taken more than he'd been given?

She showered and got dressed and then took her notebook and pencils out onto the porch. She remembered last night, sitting in Diego's arms. He made her feel…well, too much, she admitted. Safe, secure, lust, longing, a desire for something that she couldn't name.

She channeled all of that into her notebook. The dancing sparks from the fire were her guide and she created a sketch for a necklace that would have a series of rubies set in fine gold chain dancing up from a large stone.

She fiddled with it, realizing that the morning was gone by the time she finished. She felt better. After braiding her hair, she texted Kinley to see if her friend was available for lunch at the Five Families Country Club.

She wasn't, as she had a full-fledged bridezilla on her hands.

Pippa had never been the type of woman who was comfortable sitting in a restaurant by herself, so she thought about staying home. But there was no food in her fridge. So she got in the car but instead of turning toward town when she exited the Rockin' C property she turned toward Arbol Verde.

She shook her head as she realized this might have been her intent all along. When had she started lying to herself?

But she had.

She wanted to pretend that Diego meant nothing. That he was a friend with benefits, because it had been clear from the beginning that they had a bond that could almost be called friendship. But there was also something else.

Something she kept shoving further and further to the bottom of her emotional well and pretending didn't exist.

She turned under the sweeping wrought-iron banner that proclaimed the name of the ranch and drove slowly up to the main house. She saw Diego's truck and his sports car parked in the drive. Off to one side was a horse trailer.

She sat in her car with the engine on and realized that she probably should have called or texted instead of just showing up. As she started to back out of the circle drive, Diego walked around the side of the horse trailer and their eyes met.

He took his black Stetson off and lifted one hand and waved at her. She shut the engine off, got out of the car and began walking toward him as he put his hat back on and approached her.

"Hiya," she said. "I…I was on my way to lunch and wanted to see if you had time to go with me."

He leaned over and kissed her, in just the briefest touch of their lips, and stepped back. He smelled of sun, the fall air and his spicy cologne. She closed her eyes and realized she was exactly where she wanted to be. There hadn't been too many times that she'd been able to say that, but today she could.

"I'd need to shower and change if we're going into town and I have to finish giving some instructions to my staff. Or we could eat lunch here. I could have my housekeeper make us something."

"I don't mind waiting. I have to pick Penny up at two, so I need to leave by about one fifteen."

"Then let's eat here," he said. "Do you want to come to the barn with me? Or wait in the house?"

"The barn," she said. She hadn't come to his place to sit in his house with the housekeeper.

"Good. I have two new horses that I think we're going to be able to use at the riding center Mauricio and I are working on. We have secured the property and should have that finalized by the end of the week," he said. "I can't wait to get started on the building. A guy we went to high school with has a company that has been doing this sort of facility in North Texas, so we're hoping to get him to do the design."

"That sounds very exciting," she said.

"Are you okay?" he asked as they walked to the barn. He took out his phone and she noticed he was typing out a message to his housekeeper.

"Yeah. I'm waiting for the weekend, too. I should have some news by then."

"That will be a relief," he said. "It's not even my news, but I'm on edge. I hope I didn't push too hard last night, but I feel like I have to make the most of every moment we're together."

"You didn't," she said. "I feel the same way, which is why I'm here today."

"I'm glad you are," he said.

He led her into the barn, which smelled of hay and leather. The sounds of the horses were sooth-ing. While he went to discuss something with one of his ranch hands, he left her in his office. She sat there taking in all the photos on the wall of a younger Diego with his father and admitted she was jealous of the life he had.

Of the family that had surrounded him with love and let him grow into the man he was today. Until her twenty-first birthday she'd just sort of coasted along following her father's script for her life, never realizing that she was invisible to him. That she only showed up on his radar to help him further his own agenda.

# Ten

Lunch with Diego was nice, but she kept checking her phone the entire time hoping to hear from the solicitor. Sure, he'd said he'd get back to her by tomorrow, but she had run out of patience. Finally, Diego called her on it.

"What are you checking for?"

"Waiting for that email. I know it's getting later in London. I just don't want to miss hearing from the solicitor."

"I don't think there's any chance of that," he said.

"Sorry. I guess I shouldn't have come here," she said. But she'd thought they were friends and she needed someone who had her back right now. Because she felt too vulnerable and unsure of herself.

"Why did you?"

She shrugged. What was she going to say? The truth? That was complicated, and really, she wasn't even sure what was going to happen between them. She felt this bond. What could she say; when she felt nervous, her first thought was to find Diego. Just being with him calmed her down.

But that wasn't really fair to Diego. It made her feel like she was using him.

"I… You make me feel safe," she said at last. "So if I have bad news while I'm with you, I think I'll deal with it better."

He sighed and pushed his chair back before standing up and turning away from her. They were seated at a large table on his stone patio that overlooked the horse paddock and the rolling hills. He put his hands on his hips as he stared out at the land and she wondered what he saw when he did that. She knew when she stalked the House of Hamilton website she felt a sense of possession and expectation because she belonged as part of the company, not as an outsider.

Right now, she felt like an outsider.

*Fair enough.*

"I wish you wouldn't say things like that," he said.

"Why not? It's the truth," she said, carefully folding her napkin and getting up from the table. She went to stand next to him, looking out over the fields. "We said no lies."

"I thought that would be safer somehow, but it isn't."

"Safer how?"

"That maybe being brutally honest would make it easier to think of a time when you wouldn't be by my side, but that isn't the case at all. I hate that you are checking your email and waiting for the all clear to move so far from me. It's not like I have a claim on you, Pippa. I know that. Yet at the same time the thought of your leaving dominates my every waking moment and even some of my sleeping ones."

She put her hand in the middle of his back and then laid her head on his shoulder blade. Closing her eyes, she felt his heat and breathed in that scent that was so distinctive to Diego. She wrapped her other arm around his waist and held him.

She wished… She didn't know what she wished. That maybe he was just that bit of fun she'd found on her birthday night at the bachelor auction. But he had become so much more.

He put his hand over hers. "What do you expect the lawyer to say?"

"I don't know," she answered, because she didn't want to admit that she was hoping her father loved her enough to just step aside. But she had a feeling she was going to have to fight to get the right to vote her shares and she knew and expected that she'd have to prove herself. "I think it's going to be hard, but until I hear something it's so much worse. You know how when you're a kid and you hear a noise outside and you're sure it's a monster? That's how I feel right now. Everything seems like there is a monster under the bed. And I know I can fight it, but I'm not sure what kind of fight it's going to be," she said, pulling her arm from Diego and moving to stand next to him.

As much as she took comfort from being near him, she couldn't let herself start to rely on him. She needed to stand on her own. She'd known that all along, but she was still drawn here.

She was a mess. She hadn't felt like this before—never—and it was freaking her out.

"I'm used to having a plan. Every day for the last four years I've been waiting for this moment, but I had no idea what would happen when it came…and waiting even longer like this is just so much worse than you can imagine."

He turned to face her, hands on his lean hips, his hat back on his head so that his eyes were in shadow. "I get it. My brother-in-law Jose was in an airplane crash and for three days we waited to hear about survivors. We knew he'd been cheating—um, that's not for anyone else's ears—but as a family we weren't sure how to feel. I wanted Bianca to have a chance to confront him. But she never got it. So I understand how time can feel like it's moving so slowly and the wait is lasting too long."

She'd had no idea that Bianca's first husband had been unfaithful. The former supermodel was drop-dead gorgeous and one of the sweetest people Pippa had ever met.

"I won't say anything," she reassured him. "I guess you're right that you do understand where I'm coming from."

"I'm here for you, honey," he said, his voice sweet and gentle. And when he used that term of endearment, she felt things that she didn't want to admit to.

"Thank you. That means more than you can know," she said. Her phone pinged, and she looked at it and then back at him.

"Go on. See if it's the email you've been waiting for," he said.

There was a note in his voice that she didn't recognize, but she turned to her phone, picking it up and unlocking it. She'd set an alert for the solicitor's email, so she knew it was from him.

Diego stood there looking out at the pasture and paddock where his prized mares all roamed together. The breeding stock of Arbol Verde were his true assets. He sold some of the mares overseas, especially to clients in the United Arab Emirates. But today, for the first time in his life, the land didn't give him the pleasure it always had and he didn't want to try to process why.

"Okay. I need to talk to him on a secure video phone," she said. She had that edge in her voice that made Diego want to scoop her up and carry her far away so she didn't have to deal with this, but this was exactly where she needed to be.

"You can use my den," he said.

"Thank you."

He led the way into the house, which was cooler than outside but not cold. Given that it was early October, some fallish weather had arrived. This morning when he'd taken his stallion out for a morning run it had been almost cold.

His boot heels echoed on the Spanish tile and he heard the sound of Mona, his housekeeper, working in the kitchen. She was making enchiladas for the ranch hands for dinner and then she had her book club in town this evening.

So he'd be alone.

Unless he could convince Pippa that they should spend the evening together. But that felt like the worst kind of mirage. Pretending that she was his regular, steady girl instead of acknowledging that she was leaving.

"Here it is. Do you want to use my computer for the video chat?" he asked. "You'll probably have a better signal, since it's hardwired to the LAN instead of a Wi-Fi connection."

"Okay," she said. "Thank you."

She tucked a strand of hair behind her ear. Maybe it was his imagination, but her demeanor seemed to have changed since she'd received the email. She stood taller. Her motions were more controlled and the passion and…joie de vivre he always associated with her were tamped down.

He walked over to his desk, which was made of Spanish oak and had been one of the treasures his ancestors had brought with them from Cádiz when they'd come over to this new land. He rubbed his hand along the edge, feeling the past in the wood grain as he always did. Then he pushed his Swedish-designed ergonomic chair back and reached down to log on to his computer. The screen background was one of the photos that they used on the stud farm website, featuring him riding on their prizewinning stallion King Of The Night.

"There you go. I'll be back in the barn if you need me," he said.

He tried to ignore how close she was as he turned to leave. The scent of her flowery perfume wrapped around him and he felt a pang realizing this was her first step toward goodbye. He moved past her and she put her hand on his arm. Her fingers were light against his bicep.

He looked down at her.

"Thank you, Diego," she said again.

"You're welcome, honey."

He walked away before he did something stupid like pull her into his arms and make love to her on his desk, trying to reinforce the bond that had been growing between them since the bachelor auction. He'd never been one of those people who believed in love at first sight and he still wasn't sure he did, but that was what he felt for Pippa, he thought as he stalked out of the house toward the barn.

When he entered the barn, he heard his brother Mauricio talking to Brenda, one of his best trainers.

"Just let him know I stopped by. I didn't want to disturb him, so I left some paperwork on his desk back there," Mauricio said.

"I got it, Mo. I promise I'll tell him that it's there," Brenda said.

"I'm here," Diego said.

"Thank God. This one is acting like I've never been given a message before," Brenda said, full of sass the way she always was. Probably because she had known him and his brothers since they were boys. She'd hired on to the ranch when she'd been eighteen and had watched them all grow up.

"It's not that I don't trust you, Brenda," Mo said with a smile.

"Of course not," she said, turning to walk away. "I have lessons this afternoon, so I need to go and get the horses prepared."

"See you later," Diego said as she walked by him and out of the barn.

"I didn't want to bother you, but the contract came through for the training center property and I know we want to get moving on that project," Mauricio said.

"You're not," Diego said, heading toward his office at the back of the barn.

"Wasn't that Pippa's car in the drive?"

"It was."

He sat down at his desk and drew the folder that Mauricio had left there toward him. He opened it and just stared at the writing on the contract like he'd never read a word before. His mind was swirling with the fact that Pippa was in his den and probably being given the keys to her old life. Paving the very path she needed to leave Texas and return to her old life.

"D?"

"Yeah?"

"Pippa."

Mauricio wasn't going to let this be. And Diego wasn't sure what he was going to say. How was he going to make it seem like it was no big deal that she was leaving when a part of him felt like he would die without her? Dammit, he was acting like a sap. He was stronger than this. He was going to be cool with Mo. And when Pippa left, he was going to get drunk and get over her.

"So?"

"So what? She came by for lunch. I think she's leaving tomorrow."

"Damn. That's—"

"Reality."

"I was going to say that sucks. I'll be back later," Mauricio said after Diego had signed all of the papers and handed them back. "I just have to get this over to the broker."

"You don't have to."

"We're brothers, D. Of course I do."

Pippa had never felt more nervous than when Diego walked out of the den and she took a seat in front of his computer. She double-checked the number in the email from the solicitor and then typed it in. He was expecting her video call.

As soon as the camera pop-up window opened on the screen, she took a good look at herself. She used to wear a bit more makeup and look more polished, but objectively she thought she looked okay. She smoothed her hair and then made sure that the necklace her mother had given her when she turned ten was visible in the opening at the front of her shirt.

She took a deep breath before hitting the connect button.

The solicitor Simon Rooney answered the call on the first ring.

"Philippa, we are so happy you were able to call this afternoon. I have your father in the other room along with Giles Montgomery," Simon said. Giles was House of Hamilton's COO, she knew from her reading up on the company.

"I'm just happy that you were able to verify my identity so quickly," she said.

"I am, too. Before I bring the others in, I wanted to let you know that your father will not sign off on the transfer of shares until he's seen you in person. Unfortunately, he's willing to take legal action to support his position, which would tie things up in the courts whether he has a case or not. You had mentioned in your first email that you were hopeful of voting your shares at the board meeting in November. We need you back in the UK as soon as possible for that to happen."

"I'm ready to leave," she said, not quite sure that was the absolute truth because she had so many friends here. She would miss them all… especially Diego. But this was what she wanted. "Also, I have a private jet from my friends the Carutherses at my disposal, so as soon as my renewed passport arrives I'm ready."

"Good. I've sent all of your documentation

to the address you gave. It should arrive before six p.m. your time."

"Thank you, Mr. Rooney," she said.

"You're very welcome. Now, I'm going to bring your father in first. I'm not sure how much you have been following the House of Hamilton."

"Very closely," she admitted. "Or as closely as I can, being a world away. I've read about the rumored infighting between Father and the board."

"It's more than a rumor, I'm afraid. So Giles won't speak to you while your father is in the room. I'm afraid your reappearance comes at a very crucial time for the company. But I'll let your father and Giles explain their positions to you," Simon said.

"Thank you. Mr. Rooney—"

"Call me Simon," he said.

"Very well. Do you work for me or the company or my father?" she asked.

"I work for you," he said. "I hope once you've seen everything I've done for your trust over the last four years you will be happy with my work. Why do you ask?"

"I just wanted to know who was on my side," she said.

"I am."

"Okay, I'm ready to see my father first."

Simon nodded and disappeared from the

screen. She heard the sound of a door opening and the rumble of voices.

Her palms started sweating and she realized she was breathing too shallowly. She closed her eyes and remembered the way that Diego had held her in his arms last night when they'd sat in front of the fire. Remembered how safe and confident she'd felt in that moment. Then she opened her eyes to see her father sitting where Simon had been.

He looked older, she thought. Of course, he was four years older, but he seemed to have aged a lot more than that. His face, which had always been thin, now seemed gaunt, and his blue eyes were duller than she remembered. His previously salt-and-pepper hair was now all gray.

When he saw her on his screen, he stared at her face. Probably processing everything, she thought, the same way she was.

"Father."

"Pippa," he said, his voice just as low and rumbly as it always had been. For a moment she was torn between the memories of the man who'd tried to force her to marry and the man who'd read her bedtime stories when she'd been very young.

"It's good to see you again," she said, her old manners coming to the fore.

"I find that very hard to believe given that you've been hiding from me for four years," he said.

"You gave me no choice," she said. "I didn't feel like I had any options."

He inclined his head. "I've only ever had the best interests of you and your mother at heart. I thought she would have wanted you married to a good man who would give you the life you'd always known."

Pippa felt the sting of tears at the mention of her mother. "I don't think Mum would have wanted me to marry a man who didn't love me and who was a stranger."

"We can agree to disagree on that. So you're coming back. What does that mean?"

"I will be voting my shares and taking my place on the board of directors at House of Hamilton. I think we are just waiting for your signature on the paperwork," she said.

"We are. I wanted to make sure it was you. I've had men looking for you for all these years. A few times we've had some false leads."

"Now you know it's really me."

"I do know. I will sign the papers once you return to London," he said, standing up, and she hugged herself around her chest, rubbing the goose bumps on her arms.

"Father?"

"Yes?" he asked.

"Nothing," she said. What was she going to say? Admit that she was glad to see him? Ask him if he was happy she was alive? There was no answer that would satisfy her.

He walked away from the screen and Giles Montgomery got on the call next. The COO said he was excited for her to take a temporary role in the company, and once she proved herself, to take a more permanent one.

"Pippa, I'm so glad that you're coming back. I am interested in starting discussions with you to catch you up on where we are today."

"Thank you," she said. "I'm interested in taking an active role and not just being a figurehead."

"We'd like that, too. We've been at a standstill while you were missing and we are all eager to start moving the company forward again."

"I am, too, and have a few ideas that I'd like to bring forward," Pippa said.

"When you land in London, we can start our discussions, but for now I thought you might want to know more about the directors and where we stand as a company. I've asked Simon to forward you a packet with all of this information."

"Thank you," she said. "I was planning to return to the UK at the end of October."

"We need you back before that," Giles said. "There's a labor dispute with our service staff, and now that you're back, if we had an emergency board meeting, we could resolve the issue regarding pensions."

The call ended almost two hours after it had started. Her back aching, she stood up and stretched. She walked out of the den and down the hall to the family room, where she found Diego sitting in a large leather armchair watching the doorway.

"Is it settled?"

She nodded. "I'm going to leave tomorrow."

# Eleven

Diego sat there watching her as she stood on the threshold. Her arms were wrapped around her waist and she was looking…shaken.

"My father…he was all business," she said. "I guess I should have expected it. I think I've spent too much time in Cole's Hill around the Carutherses. I sort of expected the bond of family to be stronger than it ever was."

Diego stood up and walked over to her, pulling her into his arms. She stood there stiffly for a few moments and then hugged him back, burying her nose in the center of his chest. He rubbed his hands up and down her back and tried to tell himself he wasn't turned on by her, but the fact was any time he held her or thought about her he reacted this way. But that wasn't what this moment was about, so he shifted his hips so that she wouldn't notice.

"So you're leaving tomorrow, then?"

"Yes," she said, pushing away from him. He let her go. "If I can use the Caruthers jet like Nate has offered. I just have to double-check that. My passport documents are being delivered to the Rockin' C today." She rubbed her hands up and down her arms. "I have so much to do."

She really did, and not a lot of time to get it done. Diego mentally went over his schedule for the next week and assigned most of the tasks to different people who worked for him. If he did some careful maneuvering, he might be able to take a week off.

"I know this is spur-of-the-moment," he said, "but do you want me to come with you to London?"

She tipped her head to the side. Her gray eyes met his and her lips parted. "Can you do that?"

"It will take a little bit of juggling in my schedule, but yes, I can do that."

"Oh, Diego, yes, please. I'd love to have you come with me."

"Then I will. I need to make some calls and

go and talk to my hands," he said. "Do you need me to do anything else?"

"Not right now," she said. "Are you sure you want to do this?"

No, he wasn't, but he didn't want to say good-bye to her now and like this. She had other things on her mind and he cared about her. More than he wanted to think he could. But the truth was, no woman had ever dominated his thoughts and feelings the way she was…well, aside from his sister or his mom.

He might not be the smartest of men when it came to the opposite sex. But something his father had said to him when he was a teenager and dealing with his first breakup had stuck with him. His dad had told him to never let a good woman slip away until he was sure they weren't meant to be together.

"I'm positive. Do you need to head back to the Rockin' C right now?"

"I… Why?"

"I have to talk to my staff and then pack. Frankly, I have no idea what to bring to London," he said.

"How about you go and talk to your staff and I'll lay out some clothes for you before you go? It will be cold and rainy and it's not unheard of for it to snow in October."

"Snow? What have I gotten myself into?"

"It's not too late to change your mind," she said.

He walked over to her and caressed her cheek because being this close to her and not touching her was nearly impossible. He ran his finger down around the back of her neck, bringing his mouth to hers and kissing her.

"Yes, it is," he said when he broke the kiss. "I gave you my word. And to a Velasquez a promise is a promise."

She nodded.

"That means a lot to me. I mean, I can do this on my own. I'm a total 'hashtag girlboss,'" she said, making air quotes, "but it's nice to know I don't have to."

"I know where you're coming from even though I'm not a 'hashtag' anything," he said with a wink. "Just make a list of things I should pack, and then if you don't mind I'll come over to your place tonight. That way I'll be ready to go when you are."

"That sounds great," she said.

She turned and walked down the hall to his bedroom, and he watched her go for a minute thinking of the things he should be doing but knowing there was only one thing he wanted.

*Pippa.*

In his bed for the last time.

The depth of the need he felt for her surprised him and that was the last thing he wanted to dwell on. He wanted this to be physical. He was running out of moments like this.

Moments when she was his.

"I thought you had things to do," she said.

"I do," he replied. "At the top of that list is you."

"Me?"

"Unless you don't want me."

She shook her head as she leaned against the door that lead to his walk-in closet. "Don't be foolish. I will always want you."

He hoped that was true, but he knew she was leaving and going back to her real life. Soon the rancher from Cole's Hill would be a memory. He had no idea what her future held, but he was pretty damned sure it didn't involve a long-distance affair with him.

And that made him angry and sad at the same time. He had no idea how to ask her to stay. He knew he had no right to. She had to focus on returning to her old life and claiming what she'd walked away from, but it was what he wanted.

"Diego?"

He shook his head. He couldn't talk. Not right now. At this moment he needed his woman in his arms.

He pulled her into an embrace, and her breath caught as he lifted her off her feet and carried her into his bedroom, setting her down at the edge of the bed. The fabric of her dress was gauzy and soft under his fingers but not as supple as her skin.

The navy color of her dress made for a striking contrast with her blond hair and creamy skin. He found the zipper at the side of the dress and slowly drew it down the side of her body, watching as it parted and each inch of her skin was revealed.

She lifted her arms up, twining them around his neck as he pushed one of his hands into the opening, caressing her and then skimming his fingers along her back until he could reach the clasp of her bra. He undid it with one hand.

He felt her fingers on his chest, slowly pulling apart the buttons of his shirt. He heard the pop of each one as she freed him and then pushed the shirt open and down his arms. The buttons at the wrists held the fabric in place and she carefully undid each of them. He let his shirt fall to the floor.

Leaning forward, he felt the brush of her hair against his torso and the warmth of her lips as she nibbled at his pecs and then found the scar and tattoo, tracing it with her tongue. He couldn't help the growl that escaped him as he felt the sharpness of her teeth against his muscles as she nipped at him.

He could only watch her as she slowly moved

down his body. His jeans were getting tighter and tighter by the moment. He watched her tongue his nipple and his hips jerked forward as her hand moved over the button fly of his jeans.

He shifted against her, lifting and holding her with one arm under her hips. She put her hands on either side of his face and their eyes met. He wanted to think he saw the same affection and desperation in her gaze as he felt deep in his soul.

Her mouth came down on his hard, their tongues tangled and he realized he was desperately hungry for her. That there was no way he was going to be able to fill that hunger in just a week.

He pulled his mouth from hers, letting her slide down the front of his body. Once she was standing in front of him again, he pulled her arms out of her dress and pushed it down her torso. It caught at her hips, which were pressed to his. He ran his finger along the edge of her matching navy-colored bra where it met the creamy globe of her breast.

She trembled against him as her hips came into contact with the tip of his erection. He pulled her bra away from her skin and down her arms, tossing it toward his shirt on the floor.

Then he pulled her to him, letting their naked chests rub against each other. He loved the pebbly hardness of her nipples against his chest. He rubbed his hands up and down her back and lowered his head to the crook of her neck, where the scent of her perfume was stronger.

He felt her hands rubbing down his shoulders, her nails scraping down his back, and then she forced her hand between their bodies, tracing each of the muscles that ribbed his chest as she let her fingers move lower toward the fastening of his jeans.

His heart was beating so fast that he felt his pulse in his erection. He was seconds away from losing control and coming in his jeans, but he had to hold back. He wanted this time to last.

She stroked his shaft, running her hands over the ridge of it through his jeans. Everything inside him quieted and all he could think about was her naked on his bed. He needed to be inside her.

Now.

He pushed her backward and she fell onto the bed. He undid the top buttons of his jeans as he put one thigh between her parted legs. He patted her through the fabric of her underwear. She moaned his name and her legs parted even farther as he brushed the backs of his knuckles over her mound.

The lace fabric was warm and wet. He slipped one finger under the material and didn't pause for even a second as their eyes met.

She watched him through half-closed lids and sucked her lower lip into her mouth as her hips arched and thrust against him. It was only the fact that he wanted her to come at least once before he entered her that made it possible for him to keep himself in check. That and the tightness of his jeans.

She shifted against him and he pushed his finger into her, teasing her with feathering touches.

"Diego…" she said, her voice breathless and airy.

"Hmm?"

"This is nice, but I want…"

"This?" he asked, pushing his finger deep inside her.

"Oh…oh, yessssss," she said. Her hips rocked against his finger for a few strokes. He wanted to get her to the place where she was once again caught on the edge and needing more.

"Diego, please."

He used his thumb to trace around her clit. She rocked harder against his hand, her hips bucking frantically against him. She arched her back, which drew his eyes to her full breasts and hard nipples. He shifted over her on the bed and caught one in his lips, suckling her deeply as he continued to finger her. He kept his thumb on her clit as he worked his fingers deep inside her body until she threw her head back and called his name.

He felt the tightening of her body against his fingers. She kept rocking against him for a few more minutes and then collapsed into his arms.

He kept his fingers inside her body and slowly started building her toward the pinnacle again. He tipped her head toward his so he could taste her mouth. Her lips opened over his. He told himself to take it slow, to make this last. He didn't want this to end, needing to prolong their ecstasy as long as possible. Because once they left the bedroom, she would begin the final process of moving away from him, even if he was going to accompany her to London for a week.

But Pippa didn't want slow. Her nails dug into his shoulders and she shifted so that when she arched her back the hard points of her nipples brushed against his chest.

He held her with his forearm along her spine and bit lightly at the column of her neck as he used his other hand to cup her backside.

Her eyes closed and she exhaled hard as he fondled her. She moaned a sweet sound that he leaned up to capture in his mouth. She tipped her head, allowing him access. She held his shoulders and moved on him, rubbing her center over his erection.

He unbuttoned his pants, freeing himself. He

then reached for the box of condoms he kept in the nightstand drawer. He fumbled for the box, finally getting one out, and shifted back to remove it from the foil wrapper and put it on. When he was done, he came back to her and put his hands on either side of her hips as he shifted his erection so that he was poised at the entrance of her body.

He scraped his fingernail over her nipple and she shuddered. He pushed her back a little bit so he could see her. Her breasts were bare, nipples distended and begging for his mouth. He lowered his head and suckled.

He kept trying to make this last, taking it slow as he slid his body up over her so that they were pressed together. He lowered his forehead to hers and their eyes met, their breaths mingling, and he shifted his hips and plunged into her. He stopped once he was buried hilt-deep inside her and held his breath.

He wanted to remember the feel of her underneath him and wrapped around him forever.

He wanted her to remember him, as well. Long after he'd returned to Cole's Hill and his lonely bedroom and she was back at the helm of her family business.

He needed to know that she wouldn't be able to forget him.

So he claimed her, claimed Pippa as his, even

if it was only in his soul that he could acknowledge it.

He thrust into her sweet, tight body. Her eyes were closed, her hips moving subtly against him, and when he blew on her nipple, he saw gooseflesh spread down her body.

He loved the way she reacted to his mouth on her. He sucked on the skin at the base of her neck as he thrust all the way home, sheathing his entire length in her body. He knew he was leaving a mark with his mouth and that pleased him. He wanted her to remember this moment and what they had done when she was alone later.

He kept kissing and rubbing, pinching her nipples until her hands clenched in his hair and she rocked her hips harder against his length. He lifted his hips, thrusting up against her.

"Come with me," he said.

She nodded. Her eyes widened with each inch he gave her. She clutched at his hips as he continued thrusting. Her eyes were half-closed, her head tipped back.

He leaned down and caught one of her nipples in his teeth, scraping very gently. She started to tighten around him. Her hips moved faster, demanding more, but he kept the pace slow, steady, building the pleasure between them.

He suckled her nipple and rotated his hips to catch her pleasure point with each thrust. He felt her hands clenching in his hair as she threw her head back, hair brushing over his arm where he held her.

He varied his thrusts, finding a rhythm that would draw out the tension at the base of his spine. Something that would make his time in her body, wrapped in her silky limbs, last forever.

"Hold on to me tightly."

She did as he asked, and he rolled them over so that she was on top of him. He pushed her legs up against her body so that he could thrust deeper. So that she was open and vulnerable to him.

"Come now, Pippa," he said.

She nodded, and he felt her body tighten. Then she scraped her nails down his back and clutched his buttocks, drawing him in. Blood roared in his ears as he felt everything in his world center to this one woman.

He called her name as he came. She tightened around him and he looked into her eyes as he kept thrusting. He saw her eyes widen and felt the minute contractions of her body around his as she was consumed by her orgasm.

He rotated his hips against her until she stopped rocking. Then he rolled to his side holding her in his arms until the sweat dried on both of their bodies. Neither of them said a word and after a short time had passed he got up and carried her to the shower.

He made love to her again in the shower and then forced himself to leave the house to talk to his staff. Otherwise he knew he would beg her to stay.

# Twelve

"I wish I could go with you," Kinley said as she stood next to Pippa's closet.

"Me, too," she said. "I had no idea I'd accumulated all this stuff."

"Don't worry about that. Just pack what you need. I will get this all boxed up and sent to you."

Kinley came over and hugged her tightly. "I thought I was prepared to let you go, but I'm not. I mean, I still haven't decided what to do about Nate and having another baby. And you're the only one I can bitch about him to because you know I love him and am just being a spaz because I'm scared."

Pippa hugged her friend back. "I feel the same way. I haven't even had a chance to tell you about Diego or how cold my dad was on the call… We should have a standing date on video chat."

Kinley stepped back and sat down on the edge of Pippa's bed. "I love that. Let's do it on Saturday. That way Penny can chat with you, too. She's mad at you, by the way. Told me that I could tell you bye-bye from her."

Pippa's heart broke a little hearing that. "I wish there was some other way, but I can't stay."

"I know. We both know it. Even Penny. She made you this," Kinley said, going over to her big Louis Vuitton Neverfull bag and retrieving a small stack of papers that was bound with yarn. She handed it to Pippa.

"It's a book about the P girls," she said, looking down at the cover, which had a hand-drawn picture of two stick-figure girls, one with red hair and one with blond hair. She hugged the book to her and blinked to keep from crying.

"Look at it later," Kinley said. "We've been working on it since you told me you were leaving."

"Thank you, Kin. You're closer to me than a sister and I can't help wondering what a mess my life would have been if it wasn't for you," Pippa said.

"It was no big thing," Kinley said. "We found each other."

"We did," Pippa said, going to her dresser and picking up the box she'd placed there earlier. "This is for you."

"You didn't have to get me anything, but thank you."

Kinley opened the box. It contained two matching wire necklaces with pendant charms that Pippa had made over the summer during her class at the Cole's Hill Art Center. She'd known that she would be leaving in the fall and had wanted to create mementos for Kinley and Penny. "The smaller one is for the imp."

"We are going to miss you so much. These are so perfect," Kinley said.

There was a knock on the door before she could say anything else. "I'll go get it. You finish packing."

Pippa sat down on the bed after Kinley left and wrapped her arms around her waist. Who would have thought leaving her pretend life would be this hard? But then again it wasn't pretend. Everything about her time with Kinley and Penny had been real. They'd been so young and scared when they'd found each other.

She was proud of how far they'd each come. But she knew that as hard as it was to say goodbye she couldn't stay here.

Someone knocked on the wall near the entrance to her bedroom and she looked up to see

Diego standing there. He held a small bag in one hand and his Stetson in the other.

"Is that all you packed?"

"Nah," he said. "I left my suitcase downstairs. Kinley said to remind you that the jet would be ready whenever you are. I suggested that you might want to leave tonight."

She hadn't thought about that. She'd been sort of pushing off the moment when she'd have to get on the plane and head to England. "Yeah, that makes more sense. I guess I'm dreading seeing my father and not really sure what's waiting for me."

"Well, I'm just along for the ride, so whatever you decide is fine with me."

He might have been along for the ride, but only temporarily. She knew he was a crutch she was going to have to let go of. But she was glad she'd have a week with him. Diego couldn't stay longer than that. He'd told her earlier that he had a sire coming in two weeks and it was too important to trust to any of his staff.

"Let me finish this up and then I'll be ready to go. Will you let Kinley and Nate know that we'll leave tonight? I should be ready to go in an hour."

"Sounds good to me. I'll drive us and leave my truck at the airport so when I come back…I'll be able to get home."

The weight of that lay between them as their

eyes met. Then he turned and walked down the stairs. She realized how much she was giving up to reclaim her heritage. It made her mad that she'd ever had to leave it, because she realized that a part of her wanted this life she could call her own here in Cole's Hill. But another part of her wasn't willing to let her father win. The man who couldn't tell her he missed her and had looked at her like she'd irritated him.

She knew Diego understood, which made it that much harder as she walked out of the house next to him to say goodbye to everyone. The entire Caruthers clan had shown up. Little Benito gave her a sweet hug and at the last moment Penny came running outside and threw herself in Pippa's arms.

"Take care, imp."

"You, too, Pippy."

She put Penny down and got into Diego's truck, turning her head toward the rolling pastures so she could pretend she wasn't crying and that a part of her soul wasn't suddenly barren and sad.

She was nervous. He could tell by the way she kept looking out the window, but he had no words to comfort her. He knew her father had been as cold as ice on the call. But Diego had no idea what to expect when they landed in London. The private plane that the Caruthers family owned had been a boon. A chance for them to be alone as they returned to her uncertain future.

Even though he was accompanying her they both knew his stay in the UK could only be temporary. He had Arbol Verde, which he couldn't walk away from. And even if he was willing to contemplate that, he wasn't a citizen, for one thing, and he wasn't sure he wanted to live in a cold, foggy city. Though knowing that he'd have Pippa by his side was almost enough to tempt him to try.

He swirled around the mint he'd popped into his mouth at takeoff and looked over at her. She sighed again. She wore a faux-fur jacket around her shoulders. They were the only passengers on the plane. The pilot and copilot were up front, but it was only the two of them in the back.

"Are you wearing panties?" he asked.

She shifted in her seat and looked over at him. "I am. Why?"

"Go take them and your blouse off. Come back with just your fur coat on."

"Diego—"

"Do it, baby. It will take your mind off whatever is waiting for you when we land," he said.

She licked her lips. "I… Okay."

She got up slowly. He'd expected her to go to the bathroom at the back of the plane, but instead she lifted one of her legs encased in a knee-high stiletto boot. "Can you get that zipper?"

He nodded, stretching his legs out as he started to get hard. He lowered the zipper and then drew her foot out of the boot, setting it on the empty chair next to his. Then he helped her with the other one. When she pulled her slim-fitting skirt slowly up her legs, he saw that she was wearing garterless thigh-high stockings. She held her skirt up at her waist.

"Will you give me a hand, Diego?" she asked coyly.

He put his hands on either side of the waistband of her small bikini-style underpants, letting the backs of his fingers brush over her pubic area before slowly drawing the cloth down her thighs, making sure to spread his fingers out so he could caress each inch of her skin. He pushed the tiny ivory-colored panties down to her feet and she stepped out of them. He picked them up and put them in his pocket.

She arched one eyebrow at him and he just smiled at her.

She slipped the coat off her arms and set it on the padded chair she'd been sitting on and then slowly pulled the tails of her fitted shirt out of the waistband of her skirt. She undid the buttons one by one. The curves of her breasts pushed up by her demi bra became visible. When she had the buttons of her shirt undone, she slipped it off and turned around, bending over to put her blouse in her carry-on bag.

But honestly all he could see was the heart-shaped curve of her ass. He reached out, tracing the seam running down the center of her skirt. She pushed her hips back toward him and he groaned again. She stood up and turned, still wearing the bra, which shoved her breasts up and brought his gaze to them. He saw the tiniest hint of her nipple peeking out of the top of one cup as she reached between her breasts and undid the clasp. She took the bra off and held it out to him. "Do you want this, too? It'd be a shame to break up the set."

He took it and shoved it in his laptop bag and she stood there, her shoulders back, breasts bare, proud and confident. This was the Pippa he wanted to see. Not the one who'd been so worried a few moments earlier.

"Are you sure about the fur coat?" she asked.

"I am. I think you'll like the feel of it against your nipples," he said.

He took it from her chair and stood up, holding it out for her. She turned away from him and reached back to slip her arms into the sleeves. Once she had it on, he pulled her back against him, wrapping his arms around her and cupping each of her breasts in his hands. He kissed her neck as he plucked at her nipples, feeling them harden under his touch.

Then he drew the satin-lined coat closed and rubbed the fabric over her engorged nipples. She gasped, shifting her hips back and rubbing her butt against his erection.

He bit lightly at the spot where her neck met her shoulder and then slipped one hand inside the opening of her coat to tease her nipple while he continued to suckle her neck.

She moaned and shifted in his arms as he rubbed the ridge of his erection against her backside, fitting himself nicely against her. He reached lower, drawing up the fabric of her skirt with his free hand until he felt the tops of her thighs where the elastic at the top of her hose met her smooth skin. He traced one finger around the edge of the fabric and then drew his hand higher, rubbing the seam where her thigh and hip met.

Then he brushed over her mound with his fingers. She moaned, putting her hand over his, and he quickly changed their positions, putting her hand under his and using her fingers to part her slick folds.

"Open up for me," he whispered into her ear, and she shivered against him as she nodded.

He touched her exposed clit lightly with his finger, just tapped it as gently as he could. With each touch she let out a soft moan. He continued to increase the pressure of his touch, rubbing his finger around her sensitive bud and then tapping it again and again until she was writhing in his arms. She clawed at his wrist with her free hand, arching her back and turning her head to find his mouth. Their tongues mingled and she sucked hard on his as he plunged one finger deep inside her. He felt her tighten around it as she rocked her hips against his hand and cried out with the force of her orgasm.

He lifted her off her feet and sat down in his large chair, holding her on his lap. She curled her head into his chest as he kept his finger between her legs, thrusting in and out until she calmed in his arms.

Curled in Diego's arms wearing only her skirt and a fur coat, she never would have guessed she'd feel so safe. And dare she say it, so accepted.

He made her feel so warm and whole. No one else who'd known her given name, known of her life and fortune in London, had made her feel like none of it mattered, that she was enough. No one before Diego.

She reached between their bodies and pushed his zipper farther down until she could fit her hand into his pants. He was still rock hard, and as she awkwardly maneuvered herself until she could straddle him, she felt a drop of moisture on the tip of his erection. She captured it with her finger and brought it to her lips, licking it off. He groaned and shifted around. "Can you reach my wallet?"

He lifted his hips off the seat.

She felt her way around to his back pocket and found his wallet, struggling to pull it out and almost falling off his lap, which made her yelp and him laugh.

She handed it to him. He opened it and took out the condom she'd seen him put in there earlier. "What if you can't find any in England?" she joked.

"I think we'll manage," he said with a wink.

She thought they would, too. At least while it lasted between them.

At least for one more week.

As he put the condom on with one hand, she looked down at him, totally clothed except for his naked erection. She loved the idea of how respectable they might look to anyone who saw them when they were out together in public, but that secretly she was on the edge.

She could lie to herself and pretend that this thing with Diego was an affair, but she knew it was much more. He brought out parts of her that she'd never explored or thought about exploring.

Putting her hands on his shoulders, she shifted around until she could feel him at the entrance of her body and she shifted forward. "My favorite kind of ride," she said, putting her hands on either side of his face. She reached between them and took his erection in her hand, bringing him closer to her. Spreading her legs wider so that she was totally open to him.

Their eyes met as she slid all the way down on him, embedding him deep within her body. She let her head fall back and felt his breath on her breast a moment before his mouth closed over her nipple. She shivered and wrapped her arms around his shoulders, drawing him closer to her as she started to move on him.

He bent down to capture the tip of her breast between his lips. He sucked her deep in his mouth, his teeth lightly scraping against her sensitive flesh. His hand played at her other breast, arousing her, making her arch against him in need.

He lifted his head; the tips of her breasts were damp from his mouth and very tight. He rubbed his chest over them before sliding even deeper into her body.

She eased her hands down his back, rubbing his spine as he pushed himself up into her. She stared deep into his eyes, making her feel like their souls were meeting.

She was hoping he'd forgive her because she hadn't wanted to go back to London on her own.

"Pippa. Now."

His voice set off a chain reaction and she arched against him again, head falling back as her climax ripped through her body. He kept driving up into her and his hands tangled in her hair, bringing their mouths together as she came harder than before. She felt him thrusting into her and rode him hard until he grunted and she felt him jerk as he came.

She collapsed on top of him and he held her with his arms inside her fur coat, his hand rubbing up and down her back. She drifted off to sleep in his arms.

He held her closely knowing this was the last moment that they had before she would have to be Philippa Hamilton-Hoff, billionaire heiress and head of a legacy company that had been floundering in the last four years. He wondered if he'd made a big mistake by saying he'd come with her to London, but he knew that there had been no other choice for him.

He wasn't ready to let her go.

Not yet.

# Thirteen

Diego put on his shearling coat as they exited the immigration area at the private airport where the Caruthers jet had landed. It was overcast and a light rain fell. The pilot and copilot were going to stay in the UK for a week and fly him back on Saturday. Diego was grateful for that, though he could have flown commercial and wouldn't have minded.

"I'm so nervous. Simon said he was sending a car for us and I'm not sure if my dad will be at the town house that I inherited in Belgravia," Pippa said.

He put his hand on the small of her back and

walked beside her until she came to an abrupt halt. A severe-looking man stood before her, blocking her path.

"Father."

"Philippa."

Diego looked at the older man dressed in a suit with an overcoat. There was someone next to him who held an umbrella over his head to keep him from getting wet.

"Hello, sir. I'm Diego Velasquez."

"Mr. Velasquez, are you my daughter's… What are you to my daughter?" he asked.

"Her friend," Diego said.

"I wasn't expecting to see you today," Pippa said to her father.

"I asked Simon to keep me posted. I needed to catch you up on where our family stands as far as the decisions that Giles Montgomery has been making," her father said. "Perhaps we can discuss it over breakfast?"

Diego noticed that her face went very still and hard. "I can't, Father. I have a meeting with Giles this afternoon and Diego and I were hoping to get settled at the town house before then."

He nodded. "So you've already made up your mind? Giles has turned you against me."

"Father, that's not what happened. I've had four years to think about what you would do when I saw you again and—" she broke off, realizing she was getting very emotional. Had she lost her British stiff upper lip after years of living in the United States?

Diego rubbed her back and her father reached over and squeezed her hand.

"Me, too."

Just those two words. Clipped and not very emotional. But there was a look in his eyes that told her she might be missing something.

She looked at Diego and he subtly nodded. She turned back to her father.

"Okay. Let's have breakfast and you can tell me what you've been doing."

Her father looked relieved and nodded. "I'll give you both time to settle in and perhaps we can meet at the Costa near your town house in two hours. Will that do?"

"Yes."

Pippa's father turned and walked to the waiting Bentley and Pippa looked over at him. The misty rain had coated her hair and she looked cold. But for the first time he saw a sign of stubbornness in her expression.

"I can't tell if he was trying to manipulate me or if he feels something for me. But if he thinks he can manipulate me, it's not going to be easy."

"I believe that," Diego said as they were approached by a man in a black suit.

"Ms. Hamilton-Hoff?"

"Yes."

"I'm your driver, Dylan. And I'm here to take you to your town house, and of course wherever you want to go," he said. "Is that your luggage?"

He pointed to the three suitcases stacked near the curb.

"Yes, it is."

"Let's get you both in the car and then I'll see to it," he said.

Diego followed Pippa to the car and got in the back seat next to her. She didn't say anything and for once he had no idea what to do. She was giving off don't-touch-me vibes and he was smart enough to just sit next to her quietly.

"Sorry about that. I think my dad is going to be difficult about everything," she said.

"It's okay," he said. He felt bad that her father hadn't tried to hug her or anything like that. But maybe that was just some sort of British stiff upper lip that he wasn't used to. He only knew that both his father and mother had driven out to Arbol Verde to hug him and tell him to be safe before he'd left for this trip. And it was only a week. If he'd been gone for four years, he knew that his parents would start off with a lot more than conversation about the family business when they were reunited.

"He looked like he couldn't care less that I was back. I mean, I thought maybe it was because of the video chat and him being restrained because he was in Simon's office the last time…but no, he really doesn't like me," Pippa said.

Diego reached his arm along the back seat and pulled her into the curve of his body. "Everyone shows emotion in a different way."

She pulled back and glared at him. "Really? Do you think there was a shred of emotion in him?"

"No," he said. "But I don't know him. You do. You said that after your mother died he kept you in boarding schools. Maybe his way of dealing with emotion is to lock it away… I don't know."

"I don't, either," she said. "I know that was bitchy. Sorry. I'm tired and everything here is harder than I thought it would be."

And they hadn't even left the airport yet. He wondered if he'd made a mistake in coming with her now. He knew that his purpose was to help her, but it felt like the next few days were going to be hard and he didn't have anything to bring to the table. It wasn't like her family owned a horse ranch or were breeders. They were jewelers to the queen. That was a completely different world than the one he lived in.

And as the driver got behind the wheel and started to take them to her house, he realized how different this world was. He had to mentally adjust to driving on the opposite side of the road; for the first few minutes, he kept feeling like the driver wasn't paying attention. But as they got on the M25, it really struck him that he definitely wasn't in Cole's Hill anymore. There were no trucks, just luxury sedans and hatchbacks. When they exited the highway and headed toward Pippa's town house, he couldn't help but notice how pristine the Georgian rowhouses were. And there wasn't a lot of space like he was used to. He was out of his element and he knew that caring for Pippa wasn't going to be enough.

When they entered her town house, he began to get a real sense of how wealthy Pippa was. It was filled with antiques, the kind of place his mom would love. She had decorated her condo in Houston very similarly.

Pippa immediately showed him to their room and told him he could sleep.

"Where are you going?"

"I have to meet my father, and then I have the thing with Giles, but I should be back for dinner."

"Okay. I'll go with you," he said.

"I think you'd find that boring," she said.

And she didn't want him there.

"Okay. What time for dinner?"

"Seven," she said.

It was just 10:00 a.m. now.

"Thanks," she said, giving him a kiss that brushed his cheek before she left to meet her father and her attorney.

Diego watched her go, sitting in a house that wasn't his. It was about 4:00 a.m. back in Cole's Hill, so Diego texted his brother to call him when he was awake. While he was here, he needed to stay busy because otherwise he would feel like he'd followed Pippa for reasons he didn't want to admit.

He wanted her in his life. He cared about her. But she wasn't in any position for that kind of relationship, he realized. She was focused on claiming her heritage and he had to hope he was strong enough to support her while she did it.

Mauricio called him when he woke up. Talking to his brother made him feel better.

"D, I heard that there's a riding stable not too far from where you're staying. In Surrey, I think. It's the kind of operation we've been talking about setting up here."

"I'll go and check it out. Send me the details."

"I will. So how's jolly old England?"

"Cold," he said. And lonely. But he wasn't about to say that to his brother.

"Good thing you have Pippa with you to warm you up."

"Good thing," he said, ending the call after that. He had a plan. He called the riding stable in Surrey and set up an appointment for the next day. Then he got a text from Bartolome Figueras, a friend of his who was a jet-setting polo player, who wanted his opinion on a horse he was going to buy. When he texted the photo, Diego realized they were both in the UK and made plans to meet with him later in the week. Now he had something to do for the rest of the week other than sit around and wait for his heiress.

Six days of being in London and she was still trying to catch up to everything. She'd gotten home late every night and spent a few minutes trying to listen to Diego tell her about his day before she'd fallen asleep. Sometimes he made love to her in the middle of the night, but mostly she was too tired. When her alarm went off every morning, they both groaned, and she dashed out of bed and to the House of Hamilton's offices on Bond Street, where a uniformed doorman with a top hat always greeted her by name when she arrived at their showroom before going up to the office housed on the fifth floor.

She wasn't even close to getting to design jewelry or talk about new revenue streams. The power struggle between her father and the board had taken its toll on the company and she was caught in the middle. Now that she was back she had to make some hard decisions and she was ready to make them. From a standpoint of emotional revenge it would be easy, but from a business standpoint it was harder.

Some of her father's ideas were actually quite good, but all of the infighting had made the board dismiss them out of hand. On top of that, her father's arrogant ways made it harder for her to side with him.

She needed someone to talk to, but when she tried to get Diego to come meet her for lunch, he'd told her he was on his way to meet some breeders in Hampshire. She felt a little annoyed but then reminded herself he'd come with her because he'd wanted to and, really, she couldn't expect him to just sit around while she wasn't there. But a part of her—the tired and unsure part—was annoyed that he hadn't.

"My meeting is at ten and according to the GPS I should be able to get back to London by two. Do you want to meet then?" Diego asked her on the phone.

"I can't. I have a meeting that starts at two fifteen," she said.

"We could talk while I'm driving. Except that this thing keeps trying to take me down narrow single-lane roads. I think there is something wrong with the mapping app on my phone. I'm going to have Alejandro look at my phone. He's a genius with apps."

Pippa didn't really have time to chat like this. "I think that's just the way the roads are out that way. I'll talk to you later. Don't forget we have dinner tonight with the board. It's black tie. If you don't have—"

"I'm not a country bumpkin, Pippa. I can figure out black tie. Are you coming home first or should I meet you at the venue?" he asked.

There was a tone in his voice that made him sound like a stranger. It wasn't something that she'd ever felt with Diego before. Even when they'd been meeting at the coffee shop and exchanging small talk, he'd never seemed so aloof. "I'm going to try to make it home."

"Okay. I'll be ready when you get there," he said.

"Diego?"

"Yes?"

"Thank you for coming with me," she said. She knew this week wasn't turning out the way either of them had anticipated and he was due to head back to Cole's Hill on Saturday. Two days from now.

"You're welcome. I'm sorry that everything that comes along with your inheritance is harder than you anticipated."

She was, too. She had expected this to be hard, but not this hard. In fact, she was surprised that her father wasn't even the biggest obstacle she had to surmount in taking control of the company. But she also realized that for years now, she'd had a fantasy about her return: that she'd just waltz back in, present her jewelry designs and make her suggestion for a wedding line, and they'd all applaud her. Things would be smooth, as though she'd never run away or had a power struggle with her father.

But coming back to the House of Hamilton wasn't like that at all. Not even close.

"I guess that's reality, isn't it?" she asked.

"It is," he said, then she heard a horn honk and Diego curse savagely.

"I should let you go," she said. "Be careful."

"You, too," he said.

The call ended, and she put the phone back in the cradle on her desk and glanced up to see Giles standing in the doorway.

"Do you have time for a quick coffee?" he asked.

"Sure," she said. But Giles was part of the problem. As she had coffee with him, she realized that he and her father were playing her. They both assumed that she was going to back one of them to keep control of the company.

"I know you mentioned partnering with Jacs Veerling for a limited-edition wedding collection and I wanted to let you know that once we have everything sorted at the board meeting we'd like you to start discussions with her."

"I'm glad you like the idea. I've already started discussions, Giles. I know that we're going to want to move quickly to bring some new products onto the market in the second quarter next year. My father and you both have strong ideas for the company."

"We're both men who know what we want."

"You are," she said, realizing that she needed to figure out what she wanted. She'd been sincere when she'd told him she wanted to take an active role in the company, but as far as she could tell, Giles thought she'd side with him and let him move the company in the direction he wanted. She needed to find out where the rest of the board stood because every day when she walked into the House of Hamilton showroom she was reminded of her heritage and felt a responsibility to keep that luxury and quality going for another generation.

She finished her meeting with him and knew she had to go talk to the other board members because the only solution she could come up with was one where neither man retained any control over the day-to-day running of the business.

She made a few calls and then left the office, going to the meetings she'd set up. She'd been surprised to learn that many members of the board hadn't realized she was back to take her place at the helm. She spent the rest of the afternoon and early evening convincing them that she was ready to do just that.

She reflected on how she had her work cut out for her as she took a taxi back to the Belgravia home she'd been sharing with Diego. She let herself into the house and could hear voices down the hall.

She walked toward the sound and saw that Diego was entertaining two very beautiful women and a man. He stood up when he saw her.

"Pippa, I'm so glad you're here," he said. "Please come and meet my friends."

But she didn't want to meet his friends. She needed to talk to him about what she'd learned today and they had to be across town in less than forty minutes.

"I have to get changed," she said, turning on her heel and walking out of the room.

What had she expected? But she knew she'd anticipated more from Diego. She entered their bedroom and knew she'd behaved horribly to his guests and she wasn't being a very good…what? She wasn't his girlfriend. He was leaving on Saturday and she was going to be here working hard to save her heritage.

There was an ache deep inside her that she pushed aside. It was about to be over between her and Diego. She knew she would mourn, but she was going to be very busy making sure that House of Hamilton had the future she knew it deserved.

\* \* \*

Diego had been surprised when he'd run into Bartolome Figueras at the stables of the breeder he'd visited earlier that day. The Argentinian polo player turned model now spent his days working closely with breeders for his award-winning ponies. They'd met last year when Bart had come to Arbol Verde to look at Diego's mares for breeding. So earlier in the week, when Bart had texted him about the horse, Diego had invited him to stop by for drinks before dinner, hoping that he could talk shop but also introduce him to Pippa.

For the first evening since he'd been here, he hadn't just felt like her boy toy—he'd felt like he had a purpose of his own in London. But then she'd stormed in and been so rude to his guests.

Bart arched his eyebrow as Pippa left the room. The two women with him, his sister Zaira and her friend Luisana, looked at each other. "I'd say she's not too happy we are here," Luisana ventured.

"She's under a lot of stress," Diego said.

"I read a bit about it in *Hello!*" Zaira said. "I have often thought of running away and hiding from my overbearing brother, but alas, he holds the purse strings, so I have to stay."

Luisana laughed and Bart just shook his head. "We will go and leave you with your lady. But I would like to bring my sire to Arbol Verde, Diego."

"I'm looking forward to it," Diego said. He showed his guests out and then went upstairs to find Pippa.

She had changed into a lovely navy velvet gown that was fitted on the top and then flared out from the waist to her knee. She'd twisted her hair up into a chignon and had a string of pearls around her neck.

"I'm sorry I was rude. I've had a really long day," she said.

"It's all right. Bart was in the UK and I have an opportunity to do business with him, so I thought it might be nice for you to see that I'm more than just…what is it you think I am?" he asked.

He could excuse her tiredness, but this felt like more than fatigue. He had felt a distance growing between them from the moment she'd had her first meeting the day they landed.

"What do you mean?"

"I mean that you ignore me most of the time, and then when you need me, you expect me to drop everything—"

"Don't do that. I was just surprised that you had guests. I acted like a toddler and I'm sorry. Just leave it at that."

He would, except he was leaving in two days and he knew that this was something that had to be discussed in person.

"I can't."

"I know," she said, sitting down on the bed. And he could tell that she had already made her decision. "Coming back into this world has been harder than I thought it would be. Even though I'm not good at showing my appreciation, having you with me has given me the strength to stand up for myself and to try to see more clearly what it is that I can bring to the table."

He wasn't convinced. He sat down next to her, but he felt like they were oceans away from each other. Felt the gulf between her world and his very clearly. It wasn't a monetary one but more about lifestyle. And he'd never thought about that before this evening.

"I'm glad to hear that. I have felt very out of place here, but today going to meet with the breeder helped. I'm sorry that you've had a bad day."

She sighed and stood up, and he looked up at her. She had her back to him and he noticed the deep vee of her dress and how creamy her skin was. He wanted her as he always did, but he sensed she was trying to say something.

Possibly goodbye.

"It's more than a bad day. I had no idea of the amount of work that I am going to be required to do. I think I thought I could have you and the company and everything would sort itself out.

But that's not fair to you. You have a life and a business of your own," she said.

"I do. But I'm… I think we both knew this was never going to be more than this week," he said at last. He'd hoped for more, but the truth had always been staring them both in the face. He couldn't live here, and her place was in London.

He needed to be back in Cole's Hill, despite how great it had been to meet Bart today and talk about future business. His core breeding program was for the US market, and as much as he thought it would be nice to expand to Europe and maybe the polo market, he knew that he was fooling himself. He had been trying to come up with a reason to stay. A reason to come back to London so he could see her more often.

And she obviously had no time for a man or a relationship.

"I think you're trying to figure out how to tell me this is it," he said. "That the good time you wanted from the bachelor you bid on and won back in Cole's Hill is over."

"Oh, Diego, I don't know if that's true," she said.

But he heard it in her tone. She did know.

"I do. It's been fun, Pippa, and I wish…well, I wish we were different so that this could have worked, but I think it's time for me to go."

She nodded, standing there awkwardly, her

arms wrapped around her waist. She waited for him. He hoped to see some sign that she wanted him to stay, but he didn't find one.

He walked to the armoire and took out his suitcase. Chewing on her lower lip, she watched him for a minute.

"Goodbye, then."

She walked out the door and he watched her leave. Just stood there, way calmer than he felt on the inside, and let her go.

He packed his bags while she was gone and left a note and the bracelet he'd picked up for her earlier in the week when he'd still had hope that he could figure out a way to make this last. And then he left.

# Fourteen

That night in October, Pippa had known that Diego would be gone when she got back from her dinner, but it had still hurt when she'd walked into the empty house and found him gone. She hadn't opened the note he'd left her on the night-stand but had worn the bracelet he'd left. It was a tiny House of Hamilton hinged bangle in rose gold with two diamonds on either side. But that wasn't what made it valuable to her. He'd had it engraved.

*Courage is being scared to death and saddling up anyway.*

Just a little bit of Diego's courage on her wrist.

She'd taken back her company from Giles and her father and it had been too late to get any new product ready for the Christmas season this year, but they had a solid plan in place for the coming seasons.

December was lonely, and Pippa admitted she missed Kinley and Penny, who had been so much a part of her holidays until this year. Despite talking with Kinley on video chat once a week like she was currently doing, she still felt lonely and missed Texas.

"Are you even paying attention?" Kinley asked.

"No. I'm not," she admitted. She'd been looking at her bangle and wondering when the ache of losing Diego would go away.

"Well, at least you're honest about it," Kinley said. "I have news."

"Is it that you're pregnant?"

"No. Don't even say that too loud. Nate said he would give me some space and he's been so sweet," Kinley said, looking over her shoulder. "I stopped taking the pill."

"Good. You know I'm your friend and I support you, but you and Nate need more kids. The imp is turning into a diva. She needs a sibling to bring her in line," Pippa said.

"She does. Plus, Bianca is expecting, so Nate and Penny are both in a tizzy."

"I'm sure Nate appreciates you saying he's in

a tizzy," Pippa said. It was nice hearing about everyone in Cole's Hill, but she wanted to know about Diego and wasn't sure she should ask.

"He's out riding with Penny, so it's safe," Kinley said. "In fact, I asked him to take her because I have to give you some tough love today."

"What about?"

"Diego."

"There's nothing to be tough about, Kin. I told you we both decided it wouldn't work out," Pippa said. "I have been very busy getting the board in order over here and renewing contacts and working with Jacs. We're both happy with this decision."

Kinley leaned forward on her elbows. "You are a rotten liar. I know you miss him, and unless you're going to be stubborn about this, you'll admit it."

Pippa sank back against the cushions of the armchair she was sitting in and looked out at the street. There was a light snow falling and she could see her neighbor's kids outside playing in the snow. Of course she missed him. She had never expected him to be so important to her. Never guessed that she could fall for a man that quickly or completely.

She had tried dating since he'd been gone, but no one could hold a candle to Diego. It was him she wanted.

She touched the bangle on her wrist.

"I miss him. But we both made the decision, Kin. I can't just show back up in his life. Besides I have to be here and he has to be in Cole's Hill."

Kinley shook her head. "Girl, those are details. I fly to Vegas for two weeks each month and Nate and I are making it work."

"You have a kid together," Pippa pointed out.

"That has nothing to do with it and you know it. If you love him, then the other stuff will be easy to sort out. You do love him, right?"

*Yes.* But she wasn't ready to say those words out loud. And she didn't want to say them to Kinley. "What if he doesn't want me anymore? What if he's moved on?"

"You must think I'm some kind of crappy friend," Kinley said. "Would I bring him up if he'd moved on?"

Pippa shook her head. "No, of course you wouldn't. How is he?"

"Well, he was drinking at the Bull Pen last night and Derek had to break up a fight between him and Mo. Those two are both brokenhearted… the entire town says so. Mo at least deserves it— everyone knows he wouldn't commit to Hadley. But no one can figure out what happened to you. They figured that being an heiress, you can live anywhere."

She sighed. "It's not that simple. Running

House of Hamilton takes a lot of time and energy and I don't want to walk away from it."

"I think Diego would be willing to work something out with you. You know he's started a breeding program with Bart something-or-another. That hottie Argentinian. Even Nate had to admit he was good-looking."

"Exactly how did you get Nate to admit that?" she asked.

"We were both drinking with Diego," Kinley said. "That's not the point. If you love him, you need to come and claim him. He is miserable and so are you. And I think he feels like he can't ask you to come back. Plus, I miss you. Even if you were only here once a month or every other month, it would be nice."

Pippa hung up with Kinley a few minutes later, but her mind was on Diego and how he'd come here and supported her. And when she'd told him she needed space, he'd given it her. If she wanted him back in her life, she was going to have to go to him. Support him and show him that she was there for him.

She knew that Kinley was right. She loved Diego and it was time to go back and claim her rancher.

She'd need some help to do it and she knew just whom she could turn to for it.

\* \* \*

Diego woke up with a hangover, which wasn't surprising, since he and Mauricio had decided to shut down the Bull Pen again. And Manu had been there celebrating the high school football team winning the state playoffs. Things had gotten more than a little out of hand.

But it had distracted him from the fact that it was only three days until Christmas and the only thing he wanted was a certain British woman who had made it very clear she needed nothing more from him.

For the first few weeks he'd been back in Texas he'd expected her to contact him. The bangle had been a sentimental gift and he'd thought…well, that she'd—what? Suddenly realize she loved him and come running back to him?

*Wake up, loser.*

He knew she had a life in London. He'd kept up-to-date with her takeover of House of Hamilton by reading the *Financial Times* and watching the profiles cable business networks had done on her. She'd come back into her own and was setting the tone for the company, repositioning it for a new generation of high-end customers.

He'd been impressed and proud of her.

Because no matter how long he was away from her or how far apart they lived, he knew he was never going to get over her.

It hadn't taken him very long to realize that. He'd gotten on with his own business and he had Mauricio developing the riding center on the out-skirts of town. Bart had come to visit and stayed for a few weeks in November and they were going to start a new breeding program, building on the stamina of his horses and the agility of Bart's. They were both excited about the prospect.

Honestly, his business had never been better. Every night during the week he fell into bed ex-hausted. Even so, he got only a good thirty min-utes of sleep before he woke in a fever for Pippa. Taking her that last time in his bedroom had been one dumbass idea because every time he lay on his bed he remembered holding her in his arms there and it made him miss her more keenly than before.

He got out of bed and walked naked to the bathroom. He showered but didn't shave, and got dressed in a shirt and jeans. That was all he'd need. Technically it was winter, but December in Cole's Hill wasn't always that chilly. The highs were in the 70s this week.

His sister was waiting in the breakfast room when he came downstairs. Benito was sitting qui-etly next to her.

"Bianca, what are you doing here?"

"I'm worried about you," she said. "I sent Ale-jandro to check on Mo. You know they're twins and sometimes that bond helps. But you. What's going on?"

"Well, I'm planning to eat breakfast and then probably check on my mares. We have two that might foal early, which of course isn't good news."

He helped himself to the breakfast burrito that his housekeeper had left on the counter and a cup of coffee before sitting down next to Benito. He gave his nephew a kiss on the top of the head and Beni hugged him before hopping down from his chair.

"Can I watch TV now?" he asked.

"Yes. Let me get you set up," Bianca said, standing and taking him into the other room.

Diego took a huge bite of his burrito, wondering if he should just ghost while Bianca was in the other room. He stood up, pushed his chair back and was halfway to the back door.

"Don't even think about it. I'm pregnant, have already been sick once this morning, and if I have to chase you down, it's not going to be pretty," Bianca said.

"Uh, sorry, sis. I just don't want to have this conversation," he said.

"Me neither," she admitted. "You're my big brother and one of the best men I know, so I hate to see you like this."

"It's nothing," he said. "I'll get over it soon. I just need time."

She shook her head. "I don't think time will heal this."

"I do."

He wasn't going to talk about his broken heart and the way he kept waiting for something to happen between himself and Pippa. Something that wasn't going to happen.

"Fine. Are you sure you're okay?" she asked.

"Yes," he said, sitting back down. "Thank you for caring."

"Of course I care, you big dummy. Listen, I have a friend flying into Houston later this afternoon and Derek is on call, so he can't go get her. And like I said, I've been sick this morning… Would you mind picking her up?"

"Is this a setup?" he asked. Because there was something in his sister's tone that made him very suspicious. "I'm not ready for that, Bianca."

"I know," she said, putting her hand on his wrist. "Believe me, I know. It's not a setup. I just need someone to pick her up."

"Okay," he said. "I'll do it."

"Thanks. I'll text you the details of where to meet her. But I think bag claim would be a good spot."

"Will she know where to find me?" he asked. He still wasn't sure that his sister wasn't up to something, but he wasn't going to keep questioning her. He wondered if while he was there, he should book himself a ticket out of town for the holidays just to get away from everything that reminded him of Pippa.

"Yes, I told her to look for you," Bianca said. "Wear your black Stetson so she can spot you."

His sister stayed for a few hours. They talked about Christmas day and how odd it was now that she had to split her time with the Velasquez family and the Carutherses. He thought he did a good job of coming off as normal, but as soon as Bianca left he felt that gaping emptiness again and knew he wasn't adjusting as quickly as he should be.

He didn't want to keep missing Pippa for the rest of his days.

But the thought of spending Christmas without her made him sad. He promised himself that starting January 1 he was moving on. He had to. He didn't like the man he was becoming: drinking, fighting, wanting something that was beyond his reach. He wasn't that man.

It had taken her longer to get through immigration and border control at the Houston airport than she'd expected. She'd barely had enough time to dash into the ladies' room to fix her makeup and tidy up her braid. She still looked nervous and tired when she looked back at herself in the mirror.

She almost—*almost*—wanted to run back to

the departure lounge and head back to London. But she wouldn't.

Not unless Diego told her he wanted nothing to do with her. And she was perfectly prepared for him to do just that.

She was just going to… She had no idea what. But Bianca had promised to pick her up, since Kinley was in Vegas with Nate and Penny today. Bad timing on her part, Pippa thought. She'd rehearse what she was going to say to Diego on the drive from Houston to Cole's Hill.

She texted Bianca and got back a text saying to meet in the baggage claim area. She towed her suitcase behind her in that direction and then froze as she saw a familiar long, tall Texan with that distinctive black Stetson on his head, standing off to the side of the luggage carousel.

Bianca had tricked her. But Pippa didn't blame her. She guessed that it would be better to do this here in Houston. But not in the baggage claim area with all these people around.

She was trying to think of a plan to use the priority lounge to change into something more presentable when he looked up and their eyes met. Suddenly it didn't matter where they were or what they were wearing.

He was surprised to see her. That was the first thing she noticed. And then she realized he'd let his beard grow in. She liked it.

He straightened from the wall and walked toward her, and she left her suitcase and ran to him. She threw herself into his arms and he caught her. She put her hands on his jaw, framing his face, and kissed him for all she was worth.

"I missed you so much."

"I missed you, too," he said.

He kissed her and then put her on her feet. "Let's get out of here and we can talk."

She nodded. But she didn't let go of his hand. Seeing him had reinforced what Kinley had said to her. There had to be a way to make this work.

He got her suitcase and they walked out into the afternoon Houston sun. The sun felt good on her skin.

She had missed more than Diego, she realized.

He led the way to his truck and put the tailgate down, lifting her up onto it after he'd tossed her suitcase in the back. He leaned on it next to her.

"So…you're back for Christmas?"

"Yes and no," she said. "I'm really back for you, Diego. I realized I should never have let you leave. I love you. I want to figure out a way to make our lives work for us."

He didn't say anything, and she realized he might not love her.

Why hadn't she thought of that before?

But it didn't change anything. She still loved him.

He rolled his hip along the edge of the tailgate

and stepped between her legs, putting his hands on her hips.

"I love you, too, Pippa," he said. "God, I've missed you."

She pulled him close, wrapping her arms and legs around him and kissing him hard and deep.

"So how's this going to work?" he asked.

She shook her head. "I have a few ideas, but really I wasn't sure what to expect when I got here."

"Fair enough. Let's go home so I can make love to you and welcome you properly back to Texas. And then we can figure out how to make this work."

"I can't wait."

He drove her home and they made love as soon as they were on his property. He pulled the truck off the road and took her hard and deep. They stared into each other's eyes and professed their love.

When they got to his house, they made love again in the bathtub and then sat in his big bed and talked about the future.

"How long can you stay this time?" he asked.

"I'm off until January 7," she said.

"Good. I can fly back with you, if you'd like me to," he said. "Do you remember Bart—the polo player?"

She groaned. "How could I forget. I was a grade-A bitch to him."

"You weren't, and everyone understood what you were going through. He and I have been working together here in Texas, but he has purchased a large country house with a stable that he wants to use to develop polo ponies in the UK. I am one of his investors now."

"That's great. So you would be staying with him?"

"During the week I would," Diego said. "Then we can spend the weekends together. I can't be away from Arbol Verde for more than three weeks at a time."

"That will work for me. I can come here and work from Texas for a few weeks. We can sort of play it by ear until we figure out what works for us."

"I like that. Together I feel like we can do anything," Diego said.

They knew it would be hard to make their relationship work, and at first Pippa was going to have to spend more time in the UK than in Texas, but they came up with a plan that they thought would work for them.

"The important thing is that we are both in each other's lives," she said.

"Amen to that."

* * * * *

# COMING NEXT MONTH FROM

## HARLEQUIN Desire

### Available November 6, 2018

## #2623 WANT ME, COWBOY
*Copper Ridge* • by Maisey Yates
When Isaiah Grayson places an ad for a convenient wife, no one compares to his assistant, Poppy Sinclair. Clearly the ideal candidate was there all along—and after only one kiss he wants her without question. Can he convince her to say yes without love?

## #2624 MILLION DOLLAR BABY
*Texas Cattleman's Club: Bachelor Auction*
by Janice Maynard
When heiress Brooke Goodman rebels, her wild one-night stand turns out to be her coworker at the Texas Cattleman's Club! How will she resist him? Especially when the sexy Texan agrees to a temporary marriage so she can get her inheritance, *and* she learns she's expecting his child...

## #2625 THE SECOND CHANCE
*Alaskan Oil Barons* • by Catherine Mann
The only thing Charles Mikkelson III has ever lost was his marriage to Shana. But when an accident erases the last five years of her life, it's a second chance to make things right. He wants her back—in his life, in his bed. Will their reunion last when her memory returns?

## #2626 A TEXAN FOR CHRISTMAS
*Billionaires and Babies* • by Jules Bennett
Playboy Beau Elliot has come home to Pebblebrook Ranch for the holidays to prove he's a changed man. But before he can reconcile with his family, he discovers his illegitimate baby...and the walking fantasy of his live-in nanny. Will temptation turn him into a family man...or lead to his ruin?

## #2627 SUBSTITUTE SEDUCTION
*Sweet Tea and Scandal* • by Cat Schield
Amateur sleuth: event planner London McCaffrey. Objective: take down an evil businessman. Task: seduce the man's brother, Harrison Crosby, to find the family's weaknesses. Rules: do not fall for him, no matter how darkly sexy he may be. He'll hate her when he learns the truth...

## #2628 A CHRISTMAS TEMPTATION
*The Eden Empire* • by Karen Booth
Real estate tycoon Jake Wheeler needs this deal. But the one sister who doesn't want to sell is the same woman he had an affair with years ago... right before he broke her heart. Will she give him a second chance...in the boardroom *and* the bedroom?

---

# Get 4 FREE REWARDS!

## We'll send you 2 FREE Books plus 2 FREE Mystery Gifts.

**Harlequin® Desire** books feature heroes who have it all: wealth, status, incredible good looks... everything but the right woman.

FREE
Value Over
$20

---

**YES!** Please send me 2 FREE Harlequin® Desire novels and my 2 FREE gifts (gifts are worth about $10 retail). After receiving them, if I don't wish to receive any more books, I can return the shipping statement marked "cancel." If I don't cancel, I will receive 6 brand-new novels every month and be billed just $4.55 per book in the U.S. or $5.24 per book in Canada. That's a savings of at least 13% off the cover price! It's quite a bargain! Shipping and handling is just 50¢ per book in the U.S. and 75¢ per book in Canada*. I understand that accepting the 2 free books and gifts places me under no obligation to buy anything. I can always return a shipment and cancel at any time. The free books and gifts are mine to keep no matter what I decide.

225/326 HDN GMYU

Name (please print)

Address                                                                                Apt. #

City                                    State/Province                            Zip/Postal Code

### Mail to the Reader Service:
**IN U.S.A.:** P.O. Box 1341, Buffalo, NY 14240-8531
**IN CANADA:** P.O. Box 603, Fort Erie, Ontario L2A 5X3

Want to try two free books from another series! Call 1-800-873-8635 or visit www.ReaderService.com.

*Terms and prices subject to change without notice. Prices do not include applicable taxes. Sales tax applicable in N.Y. Canadian residents will be charged applicable taxes. Offer not valid in Quebec. This offer is limited to one order per household. Prices received may not be as shown. Not valid for current subscribers to Harlequin Desire books. All orders subject to approval. Credit or debit balances in a customer's account(s) may be offset by any other outstanding balance owed by or to the customer. Please allow 4 to 6 weeks for delivery. Offer available while quantities last.

**Your Privacy**—The Reader Service is committed to protecting your privacy. Our Privacy Policy is available online at www.ReaderService.com or upon request from the Reader Service. We make a portion of our mailing list available to reputable third parties that offer products we believe may interest you. If you prefer that we not exchange your name with third parties, or if you wish to clarify or modify your communication preferences, please visit us at www.ReaderService.com/consumerschoice or write to us at Reader Service Preference Service, P.O. Box 9062, Buffalo, NY 14240-9062. Include your complete name and address.

HD18

She was going to be interviewing Isaiah's potential wife.

The man she had been in love with since she was a
teenage idiot, and was still in love with now that she was
an idiot in her late twenties.

There were a whole host of reasons she'd never, ever
let on about her feelings for him.

She loved her job. She loved Isaiah's family, who were
the closest thing she had to a family of her own.

She was also living in the small town of Copper Ridge,
Oregon, which was a bit strange for a girl from Seattle,
but she did like it. It had a different pace. But that meant
there was less opportunity for a social life. There were
fewer people to interact with. By default she, and the
other folks in town, ended up spending a lot of their free
time with the people they worked with every day. There
was nothing wrong with that. But it was just…

Mostly there wasn't enough of a break from Isaiah on
any given day.

But then, she also didn't enforce one. Didn't take one. She supposed she couldn't really blame the small-town location when the likely culprit of the entire situation was her.

"Place whatever ad you need to," he said, his tone abrupt. "When you meet the right woman, you'll know."

"I'll know," she echoed lamely.

"Yes. Nobody knows me better than you do, Poppy. I have faith that you'll pick the right wife for me."

With those awful words still ringing in the room, Isaiah left her there, sitting at her desk, feeling numb.

The fact of the matter was, she probably could pick him a perfect wife. Someone who would facilitate his life, and give him space when he needed it. Someone who was beautiful and fabulous in bed.

Yes, she knew exactly what Isaiah Grayson would think made a woman the perfect wife for him.

The sad thing was, Poppy didn't possess very many of those qualities herself.

And what she so desperately wanted was for Isaiah's perfect wife to be her.

But dreams were for other women. They always had been. Which meant some other woman was going to end up with Poppy's dream.

While she played matchmaker to the whole affair.

*Don't miss what happens when Isaiah decides it's* Poppy *who should be his convenient wife in*
Want Me, Cowboy *by USA TODAY bestselling author Maisey Yates, part of her Copper Ridge series!*

*Available November 2018 wherever Harlequin® Desire books and ebooks are sold.*

www.Harlequin.com

HDEXP1018

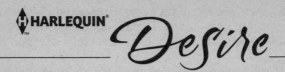

Want to give in to temptation with steamy tales of irresistible desire?

Check out **Harlequin® Presents®, Harlequin® Desire** and **Harlequin® Kimani™ Romance** books!

## New books available every month!

---

### CONNECT WITH US AT:

Facebook.com/groups/HarlequinConnection

 Facebook.com/HarlequinBooks

 Twitter.com/HarlequinBooks

 Instagram.com/HarlequinBooks

 Pinterest.com/HarlequinBooks

ReaderService.com

 **HARLEQUIN®**

**ROMANCE WHEN YOU NEED IT**

PGENRE2018

# *Love Harlequin romance?*

## DISCOVER.

Be the first to find out about promotions, news and exclusive content!

 Facebook.com/HarlequinBooks

 Twitter.com/HarlequinBooks

 Instagram.com/HarlequinBooks

Pinterest.com/HarlequinBooks

ReaderService.com

## EXPLORE.

Sign up for the Harlequin e-newsletter and download a free book from any series at **TryHarlequin.com.**

## CONNECT.

Join our Harlequin community to share your thoughts and connect with other romance readers!
**Facebook.com/groups/HarlequinConnection**

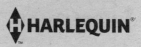

**ROMANCE WHEN YOU NEED IT**

HSOCIAL2018